NO ONE KNOWS

ALSO BY OSAMU DAZAI

*The Beggar Student*

*Early Light*

*The Flowers of Buffoonery*

*No Longer Human*

*Self-Portraits*

*The Setting Sun*

誰も知らぬ

# NO ONE KNOWS

*STORIES BY OSAMU DAZAI*

**TRANSLATED BY RALPH M<sup>C</sup>CARTHY**

**A NEW DIRECTIONS PAPERBOOK**

Manufactured in the United States of America
First published as New Directions Paperbook 1619 in 2025.

*Library of Congress Cataloging-in-Publication Data*
Names: Dazai, Osamu, 1909–1948, author. | McCarthy, Ralph F., translator.
Title: No one knows : stories / by Osamu Dazai ; translated by Ralph McCarthy.
Description: New York : New Directions Publishing, 2025.
Identifiers: LCCN 2024043479 | ISBN 9780811239332 (paperback) |
ISBN 9780811239349 (ebook)
Subjects: LCSH: Dazai, Osamu, 1909–1948 – Translations into English. |
Japan – Social life and customs – Fiction. | LCGFT: Short stories.
Classification: LCC PL825.A8 N6 2025 | DDC 895.63/44–DC23/ENG/20240930
LC record available at https://lccn.loc.gov/2024043479

10 9 8 7 6 5 4 3 2 1

New Directions Books are published for James Laughlin
by New Directions Publishing Corporation
80 Eighth Avenue, New York 10011

# CONTENTS

# PREFACE

Since 1937 I have occasionally written stories that take
the form of soliloquies by female characters. To date I've
published nine or ten such pieces. Reading back over
them now, I find myself blushing with embarrassment at
certain passages that strike me as mawkish or downright
inept. But having heard that many readers are especially
fond of these stories, I went ahead and put together this
collection of tales with female first-person narrators. I've
titled the collection *Josei* (Woman). It's a title utterly
lacking in flavor, but being overly particular about titles
is not in the best of taste either.

OSAMU DAZAI

SPRING 1942

## TRANSLATOR'S NOTE

*Josei* comprised nine of the ten stories featuring female narrators that Dazai had written as of early 1942. Only "Chiyojo" was excluded. For this collection we include, in addition to "Chiyojo," all four of the female-narrated short stories Dazai published subsequent to 1942.

Dazai died on June 13, 1948, a few days before his thirty-ninth birthday.

– RMc

NO ONE KNOWS

# LANTERN

No matter what I say, no one believes me. Everyone I meet regards me with suspicion. I visit old friends, just to see their faces again, and they welcome me with wary eyes that say, "What brings *you* here?" It's hard to bear.

I no longer want to go anywhere. Even to walk to the local baths, I always wait until after sunset. I don't want anyone to see my face. In summer, I'm mortified at how my white *yukata* seems to stand out in the evening darkness. Yesterday and today have been considerably cooler, though. The season's changing at last, and soon I'll be able to switch to my black unlined kimono. If autumn passes, winter passes, spring passes, then summer comes again, but nothing has changed, and I still have to wear that plain white yukata, I don't know what I'll do. By next summer, I want to be able to wear this gaudy morning-glory pattern of mine outdoors without hesitation, and to walk among the crowd at the festival fair wearing a

3

little tasteful makeup; it makes my heart beat faster just to think of it. But I dare not do that now.

I committed theft. I do not dispute this. I know it was not the right thing to do. However, I –

Wait. Let me make one thing clear from the beginning: I'm laying this all out for God to judge, since I can no longer depend on people. If any believe me, let them believe.

I'm the only child of a poor clog-maker. Yesterday evening, as I was sitting in the kitchen slicing onions, I could hear, from somewhere in the field out back, the sobbing, pitiful cry of a young boy calling to his older sister: *Onee-chan!* I stopped midslice, lost in thought. If I had a little sister or brother who adored me and would tearfully call out to me for comfort, maybe I wouldn't have ended up in the spot I'm in. That's the thought that got to me, and what with the onion fumes stinging my eyes and all, hot tears came spilling out. When I wiped my cheeks with the back of my hand, the onion smell stung even worse, and the tears just kept coming and coming, and I didn't know what to do.

*So, they say the clog-maker's self-centered daughter's gone boy crazy.* The cherry trees were covered with new green leaves, and irises and pinks were beginning to appear at the night market when this rumor first swept through the local beauty salon. It was during a truly enjoyable period in my life. At sunset, Mizuno-san would come to see me, and I was always ready for him well ahead of time, having changed into nice clothes and done my makeup, and I'd peek outside the front gate again and again, watching for him. People in the neighborhood noticed this, as I later discovered, and began pointing the finger, laughing and whispering. *Looks like Clog-shop Sakiko's in heat! Ha ha!* Mother and Father must have been vaguely aware of all this, but they were in no position to say anything. I'm twenty-four this year and still unmarried. It doesn't help that my family is poor, but one reason I haven't found a husband is that my mother used to be the mistress of a powerful local landowner. She turned her back on the landowner and came to an agreement with my father, and I was born shortly after she and Father began living together. We were outcasts from the beginning, and the whispered consensus that I resembled neither the landowner nor my father didn't help any. My family history being what it is, it's only natural that I'd have little prospect of marriage. Of course, with my looks, let's face it: even if my parents were wealthy aristocrats, they might have had a hard time marrying me off. In any case, I bear no grudge against my father. Nor against Mother. I'm my father's child. I believe this, no matter what anyone says. He and Mother treasure me and take good care of me, and I love them both very much. Both of them are frail, fragile people. They're the parents and I'm the child, but

I tend to do most of the pampering. I believe that all of us should treat the weak and timid with loving-kindness. Even as a child I knew that I would willingly endure any amount of pain or misery for the sake of my parents. Since meeting Mizuno-san, however, I'm afraid my filial piety has faltered a bit.

It's embarrassing to say all this. Mizuno-san is an industrial arts student and five whole years younger than me. But please don't condemn me for that; it's not as if I could pick and choose. I met him this past spring. I was receiving treatment for an eye infection at a nearby oculist. It was there, in the waiting room of the clinic, that we became acquainted. I'm a person who can be drawn to someone at first sight. Mizuno-san's left eye, like mine, was covered with a white eyepatch, and he looked extremely downhearted, scowling as he flipped back and forth through the pages of a pocket dictionary, searching for something. I too was in a gloomy mood, thanks to the bandage and the temporary loss of one eye. The new leaves of a beech tree outside the waiting-room window were blurry, as if in a haze, and seemed to emit little sparks and flashes of blue flame. It was as if everything around me existed in some faraway fairy-tale land, and with the assistance, perhaps, of this "eyepatch magic," the young stranger's face struck me as something too beautiful and precious for the real world.

Mizuno-san is an orphan. He has no relatives to claim him. His mother died when he was just a baby, and when he was twelve, his father passed away and the once-booming family business, distributing herbal medicines, began to fail. He had two older brothers and an older sister, and they all went their separate ways, split amongst distant relatives, while Mizuno-san, the youngest, was to be raised by the head clerk of the family business. He's been allowed to go to industrial school, but he feels out of place there, and gets lonely every day, and he's even told me, quite seriously, that the only time he really enjoys himself is when we're going for walks together and talking. It makes me sad that he seems to lack even some of the basic essentials of life. When he told me that he and some of his friends were planning to go to the seashore and swim this summer, he didn't look at all happy about it but, rather, downright depressed. Later that evening I committed theft. I stole a men's swimsuit.

I strolled into the biggest store in town, Daimaru, and while pretending to look for a dress, I reached behind me and snagged a pair of black swimming trunks, which I tucked tightly beneath my arm before quietly exiting the store. By the time I'd taken five or six steps outside, however, I heard a voice behind me saying, "Excuse me! Miss?" Seized with a terror that made me want to scream, I began running like mad. A deep voice behind me shouted, "Thief!" Something struck my shoulder, making me stumble, and when I turned to look back I received a hard slap across my face.

I was taken to the police box. Milling about in front of it was a crowd of people, most of whom I knew from town. My hair was undone, my knees were poking out from my disheveled yukata, and I was keenly aware of how wretched I must look.

The policeman sat me down in a small tatami-mat room at the back and interrogated me. He was a nasty-looking fellow in his late twenties or so, with very white skin and a narrow face. After grimly asking my name, address, and age, he suddenly smirked and said, "How many times have you done this?"

A chill ran through me. I couldn't even think of a reply. I knew, however, that saying nothing would only result in my being branded with a serious crime and locked up in prison. I searched desperately for words to explain what I'd done, some plausible excuse, but I was totally at a loss and absolutely terrified. The words I finally forced, with great effort, out of my mouth, struck even me as bumbling and inappropriate, but once I started I couldn't stop. I was babbling as if possessed – or possibly even insane.

"You mustn't send me to prison. I'm not a bad person. I'm twenty-four years old. For twenty-four years I've been a model of piety toward my parents. I've supported and served my mother and father faithfully. What have I ever done wrong? I've never given anyone reason to speak ill of me. Mizuno-san is a wonderful person. He'll achieve great things in the future. I'm sure of this. And I didn't want him to suffer any embarrassment. He promised his friends he'd go with them to the seaside, and I wanted him to have the basic necessities for the trip, things that everyone else has. What's so terrible about that? I'm a fool, I know. I'm a fool but, even so, I want to show the world a Mizuno-san who looks the part he was meant to play. He's a man of lofty birth, and he's different from others. I don't care what happens to me. As long as Mizuno-san finds his rightful place in this world, I'll be satisfied. I have work to do. You mustn't send me to prison. I'm twenty-four years old, and I've never wronged anyone. Haven't I done everything in my power to care for my poor, defenseless parents? You can't do this to me, you can't, you mustn't put me in prison. For twenty-four years I've done the best I can. And then, one evening, I make a foolish mistake. Does that really justify having my entire life destroyed? It isn't right! Here's what I don't understand. Does a single, careless, once-in-a-lifetime slip of my right hand somehow prove that I'm a habitual thief? That's outrageous. It's outrageous. We're talking about single, solitary event, a few seconds out of an entire lifetime. I'm still young. My life is just beginning. It will continue to be a life of the same hopeless poverty as before, I know. Nothing will change for me. I'll always be the same Sakiko

I was yesterday. But how big a setback is the loss of a single swimsuit for the owners of Daimaru? There are people who swindle others out of thousands of yen – their entire life savings, even! – and yet bask in the world's praise. Who are jails for, after all? The only people who end up in prison are those with no money. I have no doubt that most of them are honest people, powerless but incapable of deceiving anyone for profit. They're not wicked and crafty enough to get ahead in life by bamboozling their fellow human beings, but it just gets harder and harder for them to survive, and finally they do something stupid, stealing two or three yen, and end up going to prison for five or ten years. Ha ha ha ha! It's hilarious, is what it is. What a joke. Ha ha! So ridiculous . . ."

I definitely wasn't in my right mind. There's no question about that. The policeman just stared at me, his pale face going even paler, and that's when I started to have a good feeling about him. Even as I broke down sobbing, I made every effort to show him a smile. He appeared to be treating me as a mental patient, however. He walked me down to the police station, handling me as gently and protectively as you would a boil on your arm. I spent that night in a jail cell. In the morning my father came to get me, and I was allowed to go home with him. On the way back, Father asked only one thing: "They didn't rough you up, did they?"

When I saw the evening newspaper that day, I felt my entire face turn red, all the way to my ears. There I was, under this headline:

EVEN A SHOPLIFTER HAS HER REASONS:
DEGENERATE LEFTIST GAL LECTURES POLICE

This wasn't the only humiliation. People from the neighborhood began loitering and lurking around our house. This puzzled me at first, but when I finally realized they were all merely trying to get a gander at me, I began literally to tremble. It was becoming more and more obvious what an earthshaking event that little misdeed of mine had turned into. Had there been poison in the house at that moment, I would gladly have taken it; had a bamboo grove been nearby I would have quietly wandered in and hanged myself. Our shop remained closed for two or three days.

Some time later I received a letter from Mizuno-san.

*In this world, Sakiko, I am the person who trusts you most. However, you lack education. Although you are an honest woman, improper influences abound in your social environment. I have made an effort to provide a counterbalance to these, but there is a limit to what I can do. All human beings require schooling. The other day I went to the seaside with some friends. On the beach, we had a long discussion about the need for human beings to be ambitious, to aspire to something. All of us intend to become accomplished gentlemen before very long. Sakiko, tread carefully from here on. Try to atone, though your recompense be only one ten-thousandth of the harm your crime has caused; and, above all, offer a sincere and heartfelt apology to society, where we hate the sin but never the sinner.*

*— Mizuno Saburo*

*(Please burn this after reading. Burn the envelope as well. Without fail.)*

That's the entire letter. I had forgotten that Mizuno-san came from money.

Day after excruciating day goes by, and now the weather's turning cool. Tonight Father has decided the electric light in the main room is too dim and makes for a gloomy atmosphere, so he switches out the bulb with a much brighter one. Then the three of us, mother, father, and daughter, share a luminous dinner. Mother shields her eyes with the hand that holds her chopsticks, saying, "Too bright! It's too bright!" and laughing giddily, while I keep refilling Father's sake cup. *I guess happiness, for us, is a new light bulb*, I think to myself. But I can't say the thought dampens my spirits any. In fact, I'm beginning to see our modest little family, illuminated by this light, as being like a lovely vision in a revolving lantern. "Peek in on us if you will; we three are a beautiful family," is what I'd like to tell even the insects crying in the garden, as a quiet kind of rapture fills my heart.

## SCHOOLGIRL

Waking up in the morning is such a funny feeling. Like when I used to play hide-and-seek with Deko-chan and would hide in some pitch-dark closet, hugging my knees, keeping perfectly still, and suddenly she'd slide open the door with a clatter and shout, "Gotcha!" as blinding sunlight came flooding in, and I'd feel strangely awkward, and my heartbeat would quicken, and I'd adjust the front of my kimono and climb out of the closet, a little embarrassed at first and then, suddenly, angry – it's like that. Or, no, it's not like that, really, it's a different feeling, even worse somehow. You open a box and inside it is another, smaller box, and you open the smaller box and inside that is a still smaller one, and you open that and there's an even smaller one, and so on, till you've opened seven or eight boxes and finally you reach the tiniest box, about the size of a sugar cube, and you hold your breath as you lift the lid and look inside, and – there's nothing,

14

it's empty. That feeling is close. People talk about waking up suddenly, eyes popping open, but that's not how it is. It's like the top layer of some cloudy liquid slowly beginning to clear as the particles of starch or whatever settle to the bottom, until finally it all comes into focus and you open your eyes, exhausted. Morning is ruthless. So many sad feelings, all kinds of them, flood your heart, and it's awful. I hate it, I really do. I'm at my ugliest in the morning. My legs are tired and heavy, and I don't feel like getting up, or doing anything. Maybe I'm not sleeping soundly enough. They say that morning is the healthiest time, but that's another lie. Morning is gray. It's always, always the same. The emptiest, nothingest time. Lying in bed in the morning, I can't help but feel pessimistic. All sorts of mortifying regrets get balled up together like a big lump in my chest, and all I can do is lie here squirming.

Morning is mean.

"Father?" I call out to him softly, feeling silly in a way but glad, and I get up and quickly fold my futon. As I lift it to put it away, I hear myself say "*Up* we go!" and think, *What?* I've never thought of myself as a girl who'd grunt something vulgar like that. "Up we go" is appalling, like something your grandmother would say. Where did it come from, I wonder? It's creepy, as if there's an old lady living inside me. From now on I've got to be careful. It's like when you look down on someone for having a funny walk and then catch yourself walking the same way.

I never have any self-confidence in the morning. I sit down in front of the mirror in my nightgown. When I look at myself without glasses, my face is a little blurry, soft and serene. My eyeglasses are the feature I hate most about my face, but there's one good thing about having to wear them that others don't know. I like to take my glasses off and gaze into the distance. It's wonderful, all misty, like in a dream, or a scene in a zoetrope. You can't see anything unpleasant, only large objects and strong, vivid colors and light. I like to look at people with my glasses off too. It looks as if everyone is wearing a gentle, lovely smile. And I'm never tempted to argue with people or talk behind anyone's back when I don't have my glasses on. I just sit there with this vacant look on my face. I know people must think I'm awfully simple when I do that, but that only makes me feel even more vacant, more secure, and I want to entrust myself to others, to have them look out for me, and it's as though I myself have become very gentle and loving.

But I do hate my glasses. When I put them on, it's as if my face isn't a real face anymore. All the nuances a face can reveal – romance, charm, intensity, vulnerability, naivety, sadness – they're all blocked out by glasses. And trying to say things with bespectacled eyes is laughably impossible.

Glasses are goblins.

Maybe it's because I'm always thinking how much I hate my specs, but it seems to me that beautiful eyes are the best thing a person can have. Even if someone has no nose to speak of, or extremely thin lips, none of that matters if she has the type of eyes that make you feel you should live a more noble life. My eyes are big, but that's all. If I sit and peer at my own eyes, it really gets me down. Even Mother says my eyes are dull. "Lifeless eyes" – this must be what they mean by that. Charcoal, is what they remind me of. It's disheartening. I mean, just look at them. It's horrible. Every time I look in the mirror, I wish I could have what they call "liquid eyes." Eyes like green pools in a green meadow, open to the sky, mirroring the clouds that float past, reflecting even the birds. I want to meet lots of people with beautiful eyes.

Today's the first day of May. Remembering this gives me a little lift. It makes me happy to know summer isn't far off. I walk out into the garden, and the first thing I see are little flowers on the strawberry plants. The fact that Father is gone is hard to accept. To die and no longer be here – it's difficult to understand that. It just doesn't sink in. I miss my elder sister too, and certain people I know I'll never see again, and others I haven't seen for a long time. Somehow morning always brings back the past, and people I used to know, in a way that's terribly real and close and wretched, like the smell of pickled radishes, and it's just too much for me, I can't stand it.

Yapi and Kaw (short for *kawaiso*, because you can't help feeling sorry for the poor thing) come running up together. The two of them sit in front of me, and I pet Yapi – Yapi alone – and give him lots of loving attention. Yapi's white fur glistens beautifully in the sun. Kaw is filthy. I'm perfectly aware, as I pet Yapi, that Kaw is sitting there looking as if he's on the verge of tears. And of course I'm not forgetting that he's a cripple. Kaw is so sad, I just hate him. I'm purposely mean to him because I can't stand how pitiful he is. He looks like a stray, and there's no telling when the dog catcher might get him. With that leg of his, he'd never be able to run away fast enough. Why don't you go get lost in the mountains or something, Kaw? Nobody's ever going love you, so why not just hurry up and die?

It's not only Kaw I treat badly – I'm mean to people too. I find it stimulating to make trouble for others. I'm really a horrid girl.

I sit down on the edge of the veranda, petting Yapi's head, and as I look at the piercing green of the leaves in the garden I begin to feel miserable, like I just want to plop down on the ground and ... I wish I could cry. If I hold my breath and squeeze my eyes closed till they're all bloodshot, maybe I can shed a few tears. I give it a try, but nothing happens. Maybe I've already become a stone-hearted woman.

I give up the quest for tears and go back inside to start cleaning my room. As I'm sweeping the floor, I suddenly catch myself singing "Okichi the Foreigner's Girl" and glance nervously over my shoulder, as if afraid someone might be watching. It's funny that I, supposedly so mad about Mozart and Bach, would unconsciously start singing a song like that. Going "*Up* we go!" as I lift my futon, singing "Okichi" as I clean my room – it makes me wonder if it's not all over for me. At this rate, who knows what sorts of indecent things I might say in my sleep? The thought worries me but also strikes me as funny somehow, and I rest the broom and laugh to myself.

I'm going to wear the new slip I just finished sewing yesterday. I embroidered a small white rose on the breast. You can't see it when I wear my top, however, and no one else will know it's there. That puts me one up on everybody.

Mother's busy helping arrange a marriage for someone and left early this morning. Mother's always doing favors for people. She's been that way since I was a little girl, so I'm used to it, but it really is amazing how she stays so constantly on the go. You have to admire her for it. Father was always engrossed in his studies, so Mother had to take care of all the day-to-day things for both of them. He wasn't one for socializing and what have you, but she knows how to bring really nice people together. They were very different types, Mother and Father, but they seem to have had a lot of respect for each other. Ah, yes indeed, a wholesome, serene, and charming couple. Cheeky girl!

As I wait for the miso soup to heat up, I sit in the kitchen doorway and gaze out at the thicket of trees in back. Then, suddenly, I have the feeling that long ago, and at some time in the future too, I sat, will sit, in the kitchen doorway like this, in exactly the same position, thinking exactly the same thing and looking at these trees. It's as if the past, the present, and the future are all here in this one moment. This sort of thing happens to me once in a while. For example, I'm sitting in my room talking to someone. My eyes drift to a corner of the table and stop there. My mouth keeps moving, but meanwhile I'm having this weird illusion that at some time in the past I was in the same situation, talking about the same thing and looking at the same corner of the table, and that at some point in the future I'll repeat the same experience again. Or I can be walking on some footpath far out in the country and be convinced that I've been there before. I'll pass by a bean plant and pluck off one of its leaves, and, sure enough, I'll feel that I've plucked this same leaf at this same spot sometime in the past and will pluck it again, time and again.

Then there's this sort of thing: I was in the bathtub and glanced at my hands, and as I did I was certain that one day, years later, I'd be in the bathtub and I'd remember this moment, looking casually at my hands, and the sensation it gave me. It was a depressing thought, somehow. And this sort of thing: One evening I was filling the rice tub, and I felt something – to call it inspiration would probably be going too far – but I felt something shoot through me like – what would you call it? – I almost want to say "the first inkling of philosophy." Whatever it was, though, it left me feeling as if every dark recess of my heart and mind had become transparent, and I felt as if, I don't know, as if I could just sort of ease through life with a gentle kind of tranquility, without saying a word, without making a sound, like jelly oozing out of a tube, soft and pliable, as if I could just flow along forever, floating beautifully between the waves, with ease and grace. But of course I realize this has nothing to do with philosophy. Having a premonition of going through life as silently as a cat stalking a meal – there's nothing admirable, or even decent, about that; it's horrifying, in fact. If you were to experience that state of mind for very long, you might end up possessed by the Spirit or something. Like Jesus Christ. But a female Christ? How repulsive.

Maybe what it comes down to is this: I have too much time on my hands and no real hardship in life, so I have no way to process all the sense impressions I get from the hundreds and thousands of things I see and hear every day, and maybe later, as I'm gazing vacantly into space, those impressions turn into ghostly faces that come bobbing up to the surface to haunt me.

Breakfast alone in the dining room. Eating the first cucumber of the year. Summer comes from the green of cucumbers. Something in the green of May cucumbers leaves an empty feeling inside you, a prickly, ticklish sort of sadness, and as I'm eating alone in the dining room a tremendous urge to embark on a journey, to board a locomotive, comes over me. In the newspaper I see a photo of Prime Minister Konoe. What's supposed to be so attractive about him, I wonder? I don't like this sort of face. It's that forehead of his. What I enjoy most in the newspaper are the advertisements for books. The ads must cost one or two hundred yen per word or line or whatever, and you can tell that the people who write them really have to rack their brains. Little literary gems, all of them, squeezed out by people groaning and sweating to find just the right word, the most effective phrase. There can't be many pieces of prose in the world worth this much, word for word. It's a delight to read them. Very gratifying.

I finish breakfast, lock up the house, and set out for school. I know it's not going to rain, but I'm dying to carry this fabulous umbrella I got from Mother yesterday. Mother used it herself when she was a girl, and I'm proud to have acquired such a prize. I'd like to stroll through the streets of Paris with this umbrella. I bet that by the time the war is over, dreamy, old-fashioned umbrellas like this will be all the rage. A bonnet-type hat would go well with it. A long pink dress, open at the neck, long gloves of black silk lace, and beautiful purple violets on a wide-brimmed hat. Lunch at a Paris restaurant when the leaves are a rich, deep green. I'm sitting with my cheek resting on my hand, languidly observing the flow of people outside, and someone softly taps me on the shoulder. Suddenly, music: "The Rose Waltz." Ha! What a joke. The reality, of course, is just a curious old umbrella with a long, thin handle. Poor, pitiful me. The Little Match Girl. I'll just take it out on these weeds.

Ripping a few weeds from the ground in front of our gate is my way of doing "work service" for Mother. Who knows, maybe something good will happen today. I wonder why there are weeds you want to pull out and others you want to leave alone. They're all weeds, they all look more or less alike, so what makes them so different? Weeds that strike you as adorable and weeds that don't; lovely weeds and hateful weeds – why are they so clearly divided? There's no logic to it, of course. A woman's likes and dislikes can be awfully random.

After ten minutes of work service I hurry off to the station. Walking along the road between the fields, I keep thinking how I'd like to stop and sketch the scenery. I take a narrow path through the woods around the shrine, a shortcut I discovered all by myself. Glancing down at the ground as I walk, I notice little clumps of barley, about two inches high. Looking at those vivid green clusters, I think, aha, the soldiers have passed through here again. Last year a big group of soldiers came by with their horses and rested awhile in these woods, and then when I passed by here some time later, the barley that spilled from the horses' feed buckets had sprouted, just like today. But the plants never did get any bigger. This year too, since the sun can't reach them in this dark place, these skinny little sprouts will probably die, poor things, without getting any taller.

Emerging from the path through the shrine woods, near the station now, I find myself walking behind four or five laborers. As usual, they say horrid, unrepeatable things to me. I don't know what to do. I'd like to pass them, but it would require threading my way between them. I'm afraid to do that, and it would take even more courage to just stop here and let them go on until they're far ahead of me. They might take that as an insult and get angry. I'm all hot and flushed, and almost on the verge of tears. But I'm ashamed of feeling this way, so I just smile and keep walking slowly along behind the men. Nothing else happens, but the agitation I feel stays with me even after I've boarded the train. I hope it won't be long before I'm strong enough, and pure enough, not to be bothered by things like this.

Right near the door of the train is an empty seat, so I put my things there while I straighten out the pleats of my skirt, and I'm just about to sit down, when a man wearing glasses pushes my things aside and takes the seat.

"Excuse me, but I found that spot first," I tell him, but he just grins wryly and begins reading his newspaper, with an air of complete indifference. Come to think of it, though, it's hard to say which of us is more brazen. Maybe I'm the cheeky one.

There's nothing for it but to put my umbrella and other things up on the baggage rack and grab hold of a hand strap. I take out a magazine, as usual, and begin flipping through the pages with one hand, and as I'm doing this a funny thought occurs to me.

If I, lacking experiences of my own to draw on, were to be deprived of reading, I'd probably just plop down and cry. That's how dependent I am on books and magazines. I'll start to read a book and become completely engrossed in it, rely on it, adapt to it, identify with it, and try to apply it to my own life. Then I'll read a different book, and before I know it I've made a complete reversal. The skill, or rather the cunning it takes to steal someone else's ideas and make them my own – that's the only special talent I have. I get so sick of this deceitfulness, this phoniness of mine. Maybe if I were to make nothing but mistake after mistake, exposing myself every day to humiliation, I'd gain a little substance. But the truth is that I'd probably find some farfetched explanation for each of those mistakes, cleverly work it into some theory I've patched together, and proudly act out my role as the beautiful loser.

(I got that last phrase too from some book I read.)

I honestly don't know which is the real me. If I had no books to read and no models to imitate, what in the world would I do? I wouldn't be able to do anything, just curl up in a corner crying and blowing my nose like mad. At any rate, there's no hope for me, letting my thoughts wander aimlessly about like this on the train every day. All it leaves me with is this unbearable, sickeningly warmish feeling in my body. I know I've got to fix myself, somehow or other, but how do I go about seeing exactly who I am? Whatever self-criticism I've engaged in so far in my life has been completely meaningless. If I find something disagreeable about myself, some weak point, I immediately want to baby myself, to indulge myself in *that* much at least, and finally I console myself with some conclusion like "It's no good burning down your house to get rid of the mice," so it doesn't really end up being self-criticism at all. Maybe I'd do less harm not thinking about such things in the first place.

The magazine I'm reading has an article titled "What's Wrong with Today's Young Women," and a lot of different famous people have written their opinions. Reading these, I feel as though they're talking about me in particular, which is kind of embarrassing. It's funny, though, the way the contributors match up with what they've written: The piece by a person I've always considered an idiot sounds, sure enough, like something an idiot would write; the piece by someone who, judging by the photograph, looks to be smart and fashionable, is written in a smart and fashionable style; and from time to time I giggle to myself as I read. The religious leader starts right out talking about "faith," and the educator's piece, from beginning to end, is about "obligation" and "debts of gratitude." The politician comes out with a classical Chinese poem. The novelist is all affectation, using fine, foppish words. Stuck on himself.

But the things they've written are all undeniably true. We have no individuality, they say. No depth. Our goals and ambitions are misguided to begin with. In other words, we lack any genuine ideals. Nor do we have the initiative necessary to apply constructive criticism directly to our lives. No self-examination. No true self-knowledge, self-love, or self-respect. We may at times act courageously, but it's questionable whether we're capable of taking responsibility for the ramifications of our acts. We're adroit at adapting to the mode of life around us but have no real and proper affection for ourselves or attachment to the lives we lead. No true humility. Short on originality; all we do is imitate others. We lack the feeling of love for others that's supposed to be an innate human instinct. We aspire to elegance but have no real refinement or grace. And so on; there's much more, and a lot of it hits startlingly close to home. There's no denying what these people have to say.

But, at the same time, I can't help but feel that the contributors wrote these things in a more lighthearted, casual frame of mind than usual, just for the sake of writing something. They use adjectives like "true" and "real" and "innate," but they don't tell us what "true" love and "real" self-knowledge are – at least, not in any terms you can really grasp. Maybe these people do know. How grateful we'd be if only they'd be more concrete, if only they'd point the way for us with an authoritative finger. We young women of today have lost sight of how to express love, so we'd do exactly what they say if they'd only tell us, in a forceful manner, "Do this, do that," rather than "This is no good, that's no good." I wonder if they all lack confidence in their own opinions. Maybe their views would be completely different in different circumstances. They scold us for not having "proper aspirations" or "proper ambitions," but if we really were to chase after proper ideals, to what extent would they be willing to support and guide us, I wonder?

We're already conscious, however vaguely, of the Good we should aim for, the Beauty we must aspire to. We're aware of the need to improve ourselves. We all want to live good lives. In that sense we *do* have proper aspirations and ambitions. And we're anxious to find reliable, unshakable convictions. But imagine the effort it would require to realize all these things in a given role – the role of daughter, for example. Your mother, your father, and your older brothers and sisters all have their own ways of thinking, which you have to take into consideration. We young women may call others old-fashioned, but it's only talk. We definitely don't think lightly of those who have gone before us – our seniors at school, married couples, elderly people. Far from it: We constantly look up to them. We all have relatives who are forever part of our lives. We have our acquaintances. We have friends. And then there's society itself, sweeping us along with its overwhelming force. If you look at all these things, think about all these forces in our lives, the question of developing one's individuality hardly seems of vital importance. You end up thinking it's wisest not to stand out too much but to continue meekly down the path trod by everyone else.

"Mass education" strikes me as an awfully cruel system. As I've grown up, I've gradually come to realize that the ethics we're taught in school are very different from the rules of the real world. Stick faithfully to the ethics you learn in school and you'll make a complete fool of yourself. People will say you're strange, and you'll never get ahead, you'll always be poor. I wonder if there's really anyone who never tells a lie. If so, that person must be an eternal loser. Among my relatives is a man whose behavior is impeccable, who has firm beliefs, who always pursues his ideals, and who is really living in the true sense, if anyone is, but all my other relatives speak ill of him. They think of him as a hopeless case. But if he's a loser, it's only because of the way he's always been treated. I know this, but I can't bring myself to go so far as to oppose Mother and all the others by speaking up for him. I'm afraid to. When I was a little girl my feelings about something would often be completely different from everyone else's, and I'd challenge Mother. I'd ask *why* something had to be the way it was, and she'd get angry and squash any discussion with a sharp word or two. "You naughty girl," she'd say, "you sound like a little delinquent." It seemed to make her sad. I challenged Father that way once too. He just smiled and didn't say anything, but afterward he apparently told Mother I was "an eccentric child."

As I got older, though, I became more and more timid about this sort of thing. Now I can't even make a dress without considering everyone else's opinions and expectations. Secretly, I really do cherish what individuality I have, and I hope I always will, but I'm afraid to flaunt it. I want to be what people consider a nice girl. How phony I become when I'm with a large gathering of people! Blathering things I have no desire to say, things that have nothing to do with the way I feel. I do it because I know it's to my advantage to do so. But I hate it. I wish ethics would hurry up and change. Then maybe I wouldn't have to be so craven and sneaky, or trickle through life each day doing things not because I want to but because it's what everyone expects.

Ah! There's a seat. I hurriedly take my umbrella and things from the baggage rack and squeeze in between two people. On my right is a middle school student, and on my left is a woman wearing one of those shawls with a pouch on the back for her baby. Though she's no youngster, she's wearing a lot of makeup and has her hair done up in a trendy style. Her face is pretty enough, but she has deep, dark wrinkles in her neck, and she's so revolting I feel like slapping her. Once you've sat down, the things you think about are completely different from when you're standing. When you're seated, all your thoughts are spineless and unreliable.

On the seat across from me are four or five office workers, all about the same age, all with the same vacant expressions. Around thirty years old, I'd say. They're awful, all of them. Their eyes are dull and cloudy. They have no spirit. If I were to smile at one of them, however, that might be all it would take; he might latch on to me and whisk me away, and I'd end up having to marry him. One little smile is enough to decide a woman's fate. It's terrifying. Almost beyond comprehension. I definitely need to watch my step.

I certainly am thinking the strangest thoughts this morning. Two or three days ago, the face of the man who comes to take care of our garden caught my eye and positively haunted me. There's no mistaking him for anything but a gardener, and yet his face is definitely not a gardener's face. It's almost like the face of a philosopher or something. He has a swarthy complexion, but that only emphasizes the tautness of his features. The eyes are good. Eyebrows are close-knit and intense. He has a small nose, but it goes well with his dark coloring, and he looks like a man of strong will. The shape of his lips is awfully nice too. His ears are a little gross, and his hands are unmistakably a gardener's hands, but that face, shaded from the sun by a black felt hat pulled down low over his eyes – it seems a pity to waste a face like that on a gardener. I must have asked Mother three or four times if she thought the man had always been a gardener, until finally she snapped and scolded me.

This *furoshiki* I wrapped my things in today is the one

I got from Mother the first time that gardener came to our home. We were doing a big job on the house that day, cleaning and fixing everything, and we had a tatami-maker come, as well as a handyman for the kitchen. Mother was cleaning out her wardrobe and gave me this furoshiki she found. It's such a lovely, ladylike square of silk that it seems a pity to tie it into a bundle like this. I sit here with it resting on my lap and glance at it again and again. I caress it. I'd like all the people on the train to notice it too, but nobody does. If someone were to look at this lovely furoshiki, even for just a moment, I swear I'd offer to be his bride.

Unconscious drives. That is a concept that can bring me to the brink of tears. It makes me crazy when something I do or think causes me to realize the enormity of the unconscious, the tremendous power it has – a power for which our wills are no match at all. These drives aren't even things we can deny or affirm, because they're bigger than we are. The unconscious is like this big blob that covers you from head to toe and drags you around whichever way it pleases. You may feel satisfied while you're being dragged about, but that feeling is accompanied by a different one, a deep sadness at seeing this happen to yourself. I wonder why we can't go through life being satisfied with only ourselves, loving only ourselves. To see the unconscious just gobble up all the feelings and

thoughts I've had in my life, as if they were of no conse-
quence, is so disheartening. Whenever I manage to forget
myself, to lose myself in something even briefly, I'm sure
to feel a great letdown afterwards. The unconscious is a
major part of whoever I might be at any given moment,
and that realization is enough to bring tears to my eyes.
I want to call for Mother, for Father. Maybe the truth
actually lies in the very things I'm repelled by. Which is
an even more disheartening thought.

Ochanomizu Station already. Once I'm out on the
platform, I forget everything I've been thinking about.
I'd like to go back over what was in my head just a minute ago, to continue that train of thought, but it's gone;
nothing comes to mind at all. Sometimes, when this happens, I suspect there were things that hit awfully close to
home, thoughts that were painfully embarrassing, but
once they're gone it's exactly as if they never occurred
to me at all. The moment we call "now" is a funny thing.
Now ... Now ... Now ... You try to put your finger on it,
but it's already gone, and now there's a new now. *So what?*
I ask myself as I patter down the stairs of the bridge. Idiot.
Maybe there's just too much happiness in my life.

Miss Kosugi looks lovely this morning. Lovely, like my
furoshiki. That pretty shade of blue becomes her. And
that crimson carnation really stands out, too. I'd like
her even more if it weren't for the way she puts on airs.

She's too much of a poser; there's something forced and unnatural about her gestures and movements. It must get tiring for her. There's something about her personality, too, that's difficult. She's hard to figure out in a lot of ways. She tries to act cheerful, but you can tell she has a naturally gloomy disposition. Say what you will, though, she's an attractive lady. Seems a waste for her to be just a schoolteacher. She's not as popular with the other students as she used to be, but I still find her attractive. A maiden living in some ancient castle in the mountains, or on the shore of a crystalline lake, that's what she's like. Look at me, singing Miss Kosugi's praises. I wonder why she always has to be so solemn when she speaks, though. Maybe she isn't very bright. Oh dear, that's a depressing thought. She's carrying on and on, preaching about patriotism, as if we needed to have it explained to us, as if it weren't obvious and natural. Who wouldn't feel love for the land they were born in? It's so tiresome. I rest my cheek on my hand and gaze absently out the window. There's a strong wind today; maybe that's why the clouds are so gorgeous. Four rose bushes bloom in one corner of the garden. One with yellow blossoms, two with white, and one pink. It occurs to me as I sit here daydreaming that there's something to be said for human beings after all. Human beings are the ones who discovered the beauty of flowers, and they're the ones who love flowers.

Ghost stories during the lunch break. Yasubee's rendition of "The Forbidden Door," from her "Seven Wonders of Tokyo High," has everyone screaming. What's interesting about this story is that it's psychological, not just the chain-rattling, stormy-night type. We get so worked up that, even though we just ate, we're all famished again. The girl we call Madame Sweet Rolls hands some caramels round, and then we go right back to the ghosts. Everyone seems to get excited over stories like these. It's one way of getting a thrill, I guess. Finally somebody tells the one about Kuhara Fusanosuke – it's not a ghost story per se, but it's *so* funny.

During art class we all go out in the schoolyard to sketch. I wonder why Ito-sensei always has to single me out, and for no apparent reason. Today he says he wants me to be the model for his own drawing. The old umbrella I brought today was a big hit with the class, and everyone made such a fuss over it that in the end Ito-sensei noticed it too, and now he wants me to stand with the umbrella in front of these roses. He says he's going to draw me standing here like this and submit it for an exhibition. I agree to model for him, but only for thirty minutes. I'm always glad to help anyone out, but you get awfully tired standing face to face with Ito-sensei. He has such a tedious way of speaking, as if always arguing a point; and I suppose it's because he's concentrating on sketching me, but I feel as if I'm being interrogated. It's annoying. He doesn't express himself clearly, and it's a bother just answering him. He's supposed to be my teacher, but the way he gets all flustered and embarrassed and never says what he really feels is creepy, not to mention the queer way he laughs. "You remind me of my little sister, who died," he says. I can't stand it. I suppose he's a good enough person, really, but he's just too affected.

Well, look who's talking. As if, when it comes to having affectations, I myself weren't a match for Ito-sensei. I think I've got him beat, in fact, because of my skill at using my affectations in a crafty way. I'm such a poser, it's not even funny. I can say something like, "I'm a lying, deceitful monster who adopts poses and then lets those poses dictate her behavior," but that's just another pose, and where does that leave me? Even as I quietly stand here modeling for the teacher, I'm praying with all my heart to become less affected and more honest and straightforward.

Stop reading books. Your life is filled with nothing but ideas, and that senseless, arrogant, know-it-all attitude of yours is contemptible, just contemptible. Always agonizing over not having a goal in life, or how to be more positive about things, or the inconsistencies in your personality; but that "agony" is really only sentimentality in disguise. You're just indulging yourself, consoling yourself. And you seem to overestimate your own importance, too. Oh no! With a model like me, a model with such an impure heart, Ito-sensei's drawing will never be accepted for the exhibition. It couldn't possibly turn into a thing of beauty. But in the end, though I know it's not very nice, I can't help thinking what a fool this teacher is. He doesn't even know I have an embroidered rose on my slip.

Standing in one position like this, a burning desire for money suddenly flares up in me. Ten yen would be sufficient right now. *Madame Curie* is the book I most want to read. And suddenly, from out of nowhere, this sentiment pops into my head: *May Mother live a good, long life!* Being the teacher's model is surprisingly hard labor. I'm exhausted.

After school, Kinko and I – she's the daughter of a temple priest – sneak off to the Hollywood Beauty Salon to have our hair done. When they finish with me, my hair's not at all the way I asked them to do it, and it's a terrible letdown. I don't look the least bit cute, and I feel miserable. It's absolutely depressing. I begin to feel like some disgusting old hen or something, having my hair done on the sly like this. Now I really regret it. We must have awfully low opinions of ourselves, to come to a place like this. But the temple girl is in high spirits. She says crazy things like, "Maybe I should set up an *omiai* for myself right now," and before long it's as if she's under the illusion that she really *is* about to be formally introduced to a prospective husband. "What color flowers would go well with this hairdo?" she asks me, in all seriousness, and, "When I wear my kimono, what sort of obi should I fasten it with?"

She's very cute but not a deep thinker.

I smile and ask what type of man she wants to do omiai with.

"Well, you know what they say," she tells me, very solemn. "A rice-cake peddler for a rice-cake peddler." I'm a bit startled by this and ask what she means, and she startles me even more by saying that it's best for the daughter of a priest to marry a priest, that then she'll never have to worry about having enough to eat. It's as if Kinko has no personality of her own, which is probably why she seems so extraordinarily feminine. I'm not all that intimate with her, but simply because she sits next to me in school, she tells everyone I'm her best friend. She really is adorable, though. She writes me letters that she hand-delivers every other day or so, and she does help me out in a lot of ways, which I'm grateful for, but today she's so merry and frolicsome that I can't help but feel put off. After we part and I board the bus, I feel so, I don't know, so glum. And there's this horrible woman on the bus. Her kimono is soiled around the neckline, and she's got this disheveled, reddish hair that she holds in place with a single comb.

Looking at just that fierce, dark red face of hers, you can hardly tell if she's a man or a woman. And – ugh, how nauseating – she's pregnant. Now and then she grins to herself idiotically. She's a barnyard hen. And me, sneaking off to have my hair done at Hollywood, am I so different?

I think about the woman I sat next to on the train this morning, the one with all the makeup. Such a foul creature. Women are disgusting. Being one myself, I know all too well what filthy things women are, and it makes me want to gnash my teeth in vexation. The unbearable smell you get from handling goldfish – it's as if that smell covers your entire body, and no matter how much you wash and scrub, it won't come off. And when I think I've got to go through every day of my life emitting that smell, that female smell, there's something else that comes to mind and makes me think I'd rather die right now, just as I am, still a young maiden. I find myself wishing I could fall ill. If I could get some terribly serious disease, burning with fever and sweating rivers until I'm nothing but skin and bone, maybe then I'd be cleansed. Or maybe it's impossible, as long as you're living and breathing, as long as you're flesh and blood, to avoid being impure. I wonder if I'm beginning to understand what real religion is all about.

It's a relief to get off the bus. Somehow motor vehicles just don't agree with me. The air inside them is always so thick and stuffy. It's good to have the earth beneath my feet. I like myself better on solid ground. Ah, but what a scatterbrain I am! A dizzy dragonfly in paradise. I begin singing softly to myself: "Let's go home, go back home / What to see before we go? / See the onions in the field / Hear the frogs go, 'Home, go home!'" What a giddy girl you are, I think, feeling irritated with myself and hating the way I keep shooting up like a weed, growing all the time, but only physically. I want to become a nice girl, a good daughter.

I'm so accustomed to walking this dirt road on the way home each day that I've ceased to appreciate the silence of the countryside. There's nothing but the trees, the road, and the fields. Maybe today I'll pretend I'm someone who's coming here for the first time. I'm, let's see, the daughter of a clog-maker in Kanda, and this is the first time in my life to walk in the country. How would this scenery look to me then? What a great idea! And what a pathetic idea. I put on a solemn face and gaze around me wide-eyed, purposely overdoing it. Walking down this narrow, tree-lined path, I gasp as I look up at the canopy of fresh green leaves. When I cross the earthen bridge I stop to peer down at the brook awhile, gazing at my reflection in the water and barking at myself like a puppy, and when I look at the fields in the distance, I narrow my eyes as if enraptured and sigh and murmur, "How lovely!" At the shrine I stop to rest. But the woods around the shrine are dark, so I soon get up again and dash out of there with my shoulders hunched, as if I'm terribly frightened, and I pretend to be surprised by how bright it is once I emerge from the trees. Trying my best to make everything seem new and fresh, going through these elaborate charades, I somehow begin to feel insufferably lonely. And then the buoyant feeling lets me down with a thud, and I plop down on the grass in a meadow beside the road and get wrenchingly serious. I start slowly, deliberately, to think about myself, the way I am these days. I wonder what's wrong with me lately. Why do I feel so uneasy? It's as though I live in constant fear of something. Not long ago, someone told me I was becoming more and more "common."

Maybe that's true. I'm definitely not getting better. I've become so useless. It won't do. I'm such a weakling, such a coward. Suddenly I feel like screaming. As if that would somehow cover up my cowardice. I've got to *do* something about it. Maybe I'm in love. I lie on my back in the tall green grass.

"Father," I say out loud. Father, Father. The sky at sunset is so beautiful. The evening haze is tinged with pink. It's as if the light of the setting sun melts in the haze and the color runs, turning soft pink as it spreads. And that pink mist wafts and flows, slipping between the trees, creeping along the road, caressing the grass in the meadow, softly enveloping me. Every hair on my head shines with its gentle touch. How beautiful this sky is. I feel I should bow down to it, prostrate myself before something for once in my life. Right now I believe in God. I wonder what you call this color, the color the sky is now. Roses. Fire. Rainbows. Angel wings. Cathedrals. No, none of them come close. It's more holy, more divine.

*I want to love everyone.* This thought strikes me with such force that I almost feel I'm going to weep. Lying here, I can see the color of the sky slowly changing. The pink is turning purplish. I just sigh, wishing I could throw off all my clothes. I've never seen the leaves and grass looking so translucent and beautiful. I reach out and softly touch the blades of grass.

I want to live a noble, beautiful life.

When I get home, Mother's back already, and we have company. I can hear her cackling with glee, as usual. When Mother and I are alone, no matter how big a smile she might have, she never laughs out loud. But when she's with guests she'll screech with laughter, often without so much as the trace of a smile on her face. I greet everyone and immediately go around back to the well and wash my hands. I take off my stockings to wash my feet, and as I'm doing that the fishmonger arrives and says he's sorry it took so long, always grateful for your patronage, thank you thank you, and leaves a big fish next to me on the edge of the well. I don't know what kind of fish it is, but judging from its tiny, delicate scales, I have a feeling it's from Hokkaido. And as I'm washing my hands again after putting the fish on a platter, the smell definitely reminds me of when I went to my sister's house in Hokkaido the summer before last. Her house is in Tomakomai, near the sea, and the air is always full of fish smells. I can still vividly recall her standing alone in that spacious kitchen one evening, skillfully preparing fish for dinner with those alabaster, ladylike hands of hers. And I felt such a longing for her, wanting to have her care for me and pamper me as she used to; but she'd already given birth to Toshi by then and was no longer mine. This realization was like a cold draft sweeping through me. Knowing I couldn't just go up and put my arms around her slender shoulders and hug her, I felt so lonely I could have died, just standing there in one corner of that dimly lit kitchen, watching those breathtaking, gentle, white fingertips working away. I miss the past so much, all of it. Blood is a mysterious thing. With people who aren't related to you, the farther away they are, the less you feel for them and the easier it is to forget them. But when you're separated from blood relations, you just miss them more and more and remember all the beautiful things about them.

The wild olives beside the well are a faint pink now. They may be ready to eat in a couple of weeks or so. Last year, it was so funny. I was picking the wild olives and eating them one evening, and Yapi was sitting there watching me until I felt sorry for him and gave him one. And he ate it! So I gave him a couple more, and he ate those too. It was funny to watch, so I shook the tree, and olives came plopping down all over the place, and Yapi was gobbling them up like crazy. Stupid dog. Who ever heard of a dog eating wild olives? I was standing on tiptoe picking the olives and eating them while down below, Yapi was rooting for them on the ground. Remembering that time and laughing to myself, I start to wonder where he is.

"Yapi!"

He comes trotting cockily around from the front. Suddenly he strikes me as so adorable that I have to grit my teeth. I grab hold of his tail and squeeze, and he gently bites my hand. I feel tears welling up, and I smack him on the head. It doesn't bother him at all, though; he just turns and starts noisily lapping water from the well.

I go to my room. The electric light is shining softly. It's so quiet. Father is gone. Without Father here it's as if we have this great, empty space in the house. It's enough to make you shudder sometimes. After changing into a kimono and giving the rose on my discarded slip a gentle kiss, I sit down in front of the mirror. And just then, from the living room, much to my disgust, Mother and her friends burst into a great roar of laughter. When Mother and I are alone everything's fine, but when we have company, she seems so distant from me, so cold and formal, and that's when I miss Father the most.

When I peer into the mirror, I'm taken aback by how vivacious I look. This face is a stranger to me. It has absolutely nothing to do with these feelings of mine, this sadness and pain. It's living a life of its own. Though I'm not wearing rouge today, my cheeks are bright pink, and my lips are small and red and shiny. I look adorable. I take off my glasses and smile softly. My eyes are very nice right now. Clear as a blue, blue sky. Maybe it's because I gazed at that beautiful evening sky for so long. Hooray.

I go to the kitchen practically floating on air, but as I'm washing the rice I begin to feel sad again. I long for the old house in Koganei. I miss it so much, it wrings my heart. Father was there, in that nice old house, and so was my sister. And Mother was younger then. I'd come home from school, and Mother and my sister would be sitting in the kitchen or the living room, happily chatting away about one thing or another. They'd give me a snack, and both of them would fuss over me. Sometimes I'd start an argument with my sister, which would earn me a scolding, and then I'd run outside, jump on my bicycle, and ride far away. I'd always come back by dinnertime, though, and we'd all have a peaceful and pleasant meal together. It really was a happy time. I didn't spend my days thinking about myself, and I didn't feel so nasty and awkward all the time; I had only to let them look after me. What tremendous privileges I enjoyed! And without thinking anything of it. No worries, no loneliness, no suffering. Father was a splendid father. My sister was gentle and kind, and I was always trailing after her. But as I gradually got bigger and found out all these disgusting things about myself, the privileges began to vanish, leaving me here naked and unprotected and ugly. So ugly. I wouldn't even be capable of letting anyone baby me now. All I do is brood, and feel more and more hurt. My sister went and got married. Father's gone. The only ones left are Mother and me. Mother must be awfully lonely too. Not long ago she gave me a little talking-to. "From here on in," she said, "there's nothing for me to enjoy in life. Even watching you grow up – to be completely honest, I don't really take much pleasure in it anymore. Forgive me. You must understand: it's natural and proper that I have no real happiness, now that your father's gone." She tells me that when the mosquitoes come out, it makes her think of Father; when she's unstitching something, she remembers Father; and especially when she's drinking a cup of delicious tea, she always reminisces about Father. No matter how much I try to console her and talk with her, it's not the same, I'm not Father. The love between husband and wife must be the strongest bond in the world, stronger and more precious than even the love that blood relatives feel.

A blush warms my cheeks at such intimate thoughts, and I run a wet hand through my hair. Washing the rice, swishing it around, I begin to think of Mother as the sweetest, most lovable person, and to remind myself how important it is to take good care of her. The first thing I've got to do is get rid of this wave I had them put in my hair, and then I'll let it grow longer. Mother has never liked me with bobbed hair; it ought to make her happy if I let it grow really long and do it up nice. But then again, I hate to go that far just out of consideration for Mother. It'd be sort of creepy. Come to think of it, much of the anxiety I feel these days has a lot to do with Mother. I want to be a good daughter, just the kind of girl she'd like me to be, but I don't like the idea of trying to please her in such queer ways. It would be best if I didn't have to do or say anything, if she would just understand me and trust me. However headstrong I may be, I'll never do anything to invite people's ridicule, and no matter how hard it may be at times, no matter how lonely I may get, I'll always be on my guard against making any of the really bad mistakes. And I do love Mother. I love her and I love my life in this house with her, so if she'd just have faith in me and not worry about anything, if she'd just relax and be a bit more happy-go-lucky, everything would be fine. I know I'd make her proud of me. I'd work my fingers to the bone for her. Even now, that's the greatest joy in my life, and it's all I really want to do with my life. But Mother doesn't have any confidence in me; she still treats me like a child, and she loves it when I say something childish. Not long ago I took out an old ukulele and started fooling around, plinking the strings, and Mother, looking perfectly ecstatic, said, "What's that? Rain? I hear raindrops," teasing me as if I were a toddler earnestly trying to play the thing. This little incident left me feeling completely forlorn. I just wanted to weep. Mother, I'm an adult now. I already know all about the world, and people. Feel free to talk to me about anything, anything at all. Even our household finances, for example – if you would just tell me everything, if you would say to me, "Look, this is how things stand, so you're going to have to do your part too," I'd never bother you about new shoes and things like that. I'd be a properly thrifty, frugal daughter. That's really, truly the truth. And yet . . .

Ah! I start snickering to myself, remembering that there was a song with that title, "And Yet," and suddenly I realize I'm standing here with both hands stuck in the rice pot, daydreaming like an idiot.

This won't do. I've got to get dinner ready for the guests. I wonder what I should do with this big fish. For starters I cut it into three pieces and soak them in miso, which always adds to the flavor. When it comes to cooking, you have to rely on intuition. There are a few cucumbers left, so I'll put them in a simple sauce of sake, soy, and vinegar. Then my famous omelet. Then, let's see, one more dish ... Oh, of course: my rococo cuisine. This is something I dreamed up myself, don't you know. On each plate I place a bit of ham, egg, parsley, cabbage, spinach, everything we have in the way of leftovers, a full spectrum of colors, laying them out beautifully with the hands of an artist. It's a dish that's easy to prepare, it's economical, and it's not the least bit delicious, but it lends an atmosphere of gaiety and extravagance to the dinner table and makes it appear as if you've laid out a real feast. Behind a hillock of egg grows a green carpet of parsley, beside which a red coral reef of ham peeks out, all resting on a bed of cabbage leaves arranged on the plate like a yellow peony, or a feather fan. Spinach adds a deep-green pasture, or tidal waters. Put two or three of these plates on the table, and suddenly the guests have visions of eighteenth-century France. All right, that's overstating things a bit, but since I'm incapable of making anything really delicious, the least I can do is serve up something that's so attractive to the eye that the guests are dazzled into thinking it's actually tasty. Appearances come first in serving up a meal. You can get away with just about anything if it looks good. But mind you, this rococo cuisine requires an artistic eye. Unless you're much more sensitive to color combinations than the average person, you're sure to fail. You need at least as much delicacy as yours truly has, anyway. When I looked up "rococo" in the dictionary awhile back, it was defined as "an ornamental style emphasizing the florid and gorgeous but lacking substance." I couldn't help but laugh – it was so perfect. How could anything beautiful have "substance," anyway? Pure beauty is always without meaning or morality. It's obvious. That's why I'm all in favor of rococo.

As often happens when I'm cooking, however, while I'm sampling this and tasting that, I'm slowly overcome by this horrible sense of emptiness. It's as if all the exertion has reached a saturation point. My spirits plummet, and suddenly I'm dead tired and depressed, thinking: *Enough!* Who cares how anything turns out? I just give up and throw everything together any old way, with no regard for how it might taste or look, and serve it to the guests with a perfectly sullen expression on my face.

Today's guests are particularly depressing. Mr. and Mrs. Imaida from Omori and their seven-year-old son, Yoshio. Mr. Imaida is almost forty, but he has this very white, pretty-boy type of complexion. Ick. And why does he have to smoke Shikishima cigarettes? There's something indecent about cigarettes with mouthpieces. If a man smokes Shikishimas, you begin to have doubts about his character. He tilts his head back and blows the smoke out at the ceiling, going, "Aha, aha, I see." He's a teacher at night school. His wife is this small, timid person, and she's a boorish sort. The silliest things are enough to make her double over with laughter on her cushion, twisting her body around and nearly pressing her face against the tatami. What's so funny? The worst part is, she seems to be under the mistaken impression that it's in good taste to overreact like that, to fall down laughing. I wonder if people like this don't make up the least desirable class in society today. The most sordid class. "Petit bourgeois," is that what you'd call them? Even the little boy is precocious in a queer sort of way. There's not a trace of natural, spontaneous playfulness about him.

Though I'm thinking all these things, I keep it all inside and bow to the guests and laugh and chat and say how cute Yoshio is, patting his head, deceiving everyone with my lies. Doesn't that make even people like the Imaidas more pure of heart than I am? Everyone praises my cooking as they dig into the rococo cuisine, and it makes me feel so wretched and angry I want to burst into tears. I force myself to looked pleased, however, and dig in with the rest of them, but Mrs. Imaida won't stop mindlessly flattering me, so much that I can't help but be repulsed by it and finally brace myself and think, all right, that's it, no more lies.

"Please. This food isn't the least bit delicious. It's just

emergency rations, really, since we didn't have anything else to serve."

I only meant to tell the truth, but Mr. and Mrs. Imaida laugh merrily, all but clapping their hands. "Emergency rations! That's a good one!" It's so exasperating, I want to dash my chopsticks and bowl to the floor and howl at the top of my lungs. But I hold it all inside and force myself to produce a simpering grin. Then Mother chimes in.

"This child is really getting to be quite a help around here." Though she knows perfectly well how awful I feel, she chooses to go along with the Imaidas by chuckling and saying something silly like this. Mother, there's no need to go out of your way to align yourself with people like this. Mother isn't Mother when she has guests. She's just this weak-willed woman. Mother, you don't have to kowtow to anyone simply because Father's gone. I feel so miserable I can't even speak. Go home, Imaidas. Please go home. My father is a fine man, a gentle man, a man of noble and lofty character. If you think you can make fools of us merely because Father's not here, you can just leave right now. I really feel like saying that to them. But of course I'm too much of a coward, and instead I cut a slice of ham for Yoshio and serve the Missus some pickled vegetables.

As soon as dinner's over, I retreat to the kitchen and start cleaning up. I wanted to be alone as soon as possible. It's not that I'm being snobbish, but I don't see why

I should have to force myself to chatter and cackle with those people. There's absolutely no need to be polite to – or toady to, rather – people like that. I've had it. No more of this. I did my best. Even Mother seemed happy, didn't she, to see how I restrained myself and acted so amiable and courteous? Is that all you have to do, I wonder? I don't know which is better: to distinguish clearly between your social self and your real self and go about coping with everything in a methodical, cheerful way; or to never conceal or lose sight of your real self, even if people ridicule you for it. I have to admit I envy people who never doubt themselves and spend their whole lives among others who are equally meek and gentle and warm. As far as hardship goes, if you can get through your life without experiencing it, so much the better; there's no need to go out of your way to seek hardship.

Of course, it's certainly true that it's good to do things for others, even if it means stifling your true feelings, but if I thought I had to go through every day from now on forcing myself to smile at people like the Imaidas, and listening and responding to everything they say, I believe I'd go insane. I often think I'd never be able to make it in prison. I know that's a funny thought, but it's true. Prison? I couldn't even make it as someone's maid. Or as a wife. No, wait – being a wife would be different. Once you've made up your mind to devote yourself to someone until death, then no matter how much you toil and suffer, you're bound to feel that life is worth living, that there's always hope. It's only natural. Even I could become an admirable wife. I'd be busy as a bee from morning to night. Forever scrubbing away at the laundry – because nothing is more unpleasant than a great pile of dirty clothing. I get so discombobulated when the laundry piles up, it's as if I'm on the verge of hysteria. I feel I'll die if I don't get the washing done. And once I've washed every last item and hung everything up to dry, I feel that if I *were* to die now, at least I could rest in peace.

The Imaidas are leaving. Mother's going with them, saying they have some sort of business to take care of together. That's Mother for you. As for the Imaidas, using her like that (and it's not the first time), I'd like to give them a good thrashing for having such gall. After seeing the four of them off at the front gate, I stand here alone gazing at the twilit street and wanting to cry.

In the mailbox are the evening paper and two postcards. One is for Mother, but it's only an announcement from the Matsuzaka-ya store for a summer clothing sale. The other one is for me, from my cousin Junji. It's just a short note: "I'm being transferred to the regiment in Maebashi. Give my regards to your mother." I know that life in the army is far from wonderful, even for commissioned officers, but even so, I sometimes envy soldiers the discipline forced upon them, the rigorous daily routine in which not a second is wasted, and everything is done according to some regulation. In a way it must put you at ease. As for me, if I don't feel like doing anything at all, I don't have to; yet I'm in a position where I could do all sorts of bad, terrible things if I wanted. If I want to study, I have all the time in the world to do so; but if I decide to be selfish and immoral, my most extravagant desires might be fulfilled. What a help it would be for my state of mind if someone were to put limits on what I could do. I'd actually be grateful for restrictions like that. I read in some magazine that there's just one thing soldiers on the front crave: a good night's sleep. I sympathize with the soldiers, but this made me envious of them as well. To be able to make a clean break from this vicious cycle of vile, complicated reflections, this meaningless flood of thoughts, and to be in a state of longing only to sleep – it moves me just to think about the purity and simplicity of such a life. If I could experience military life just once, and go through that sort of severe training, maybe I'd become somewhat more well-adjusted and attractive. Of course, some people don't need to go through the military to become honest and unaffected – Junji's younger brother Shin, for example – but I'm not like that; I'm a bad girl with many terrible character flaws. Shin is the same age as I, but he's such a good person you can't help but wonder how he got that way. He's my favorite relative, maybe my favorite person in the whole world. Shin is blind. Imagine losing your sight when you're so young. What would it be like on a quiet night like this, alone in your room? The rest of us, when we feel miserable, we can console ourselves by reading a book or looking at the scenery, but Shin can't. All he can do is accept his fate. Shin always studied harder than anybody, and he was good at tennis and swimming, so just think how painful and sad it must be for him now. Last night I was thinking about Shin, and after I got in bed I tried lying there awake with my eyes closed for five minutes. Even lying down, five minutes seemed like an eternity. But Shin never sees anything, morning noon and night, day after day, month after month. If he'd complain once in a while, or lose his temper, or say something selfish, I honestly think I'd be happy for him, but he never does. I've never heard him complain or say anything bad about anyone. He has this cheerful way of talking, and such an ingenuous, detached expression on his face. It really gets to you.

While I'm thinking about all this, I clean the floor in the sitting room, and then I light the fire for the bath. As I wait for the water to heat, I sit on the wooden crate and do my homework by the light of the burning coals. Even when I've finished it all, the bath still isn't ready, so I decide to start reading *A Strange Tale from East of the River* again. There's definitely nothing vile or hateful about the story itself, but here and there the author's posturing stands out, and he seems, I don't know, I guess you'd have to say antiquated, and just a bit "off." Well, he's an old man; maybe that's why. But foreign writers, when they get old, they only seem to have an even bolder, more indulgent love for their subjects, and it doesn't make them come across as affected – quite the opposite, in fact. Still, I wonder if this isn't one of the better class of Japanese literary works. There's a refreshing, relatively honest, quiet kind of resignation underlying the story. It's the most mellow of Kafu's stories, and I do like it. He seems to have an awfully strong sense of moral responsibility. It's as if, in a lot of his works, he's so concerned with Japanese morality that he ends up defying it, rebelling in a forced, unnatural way. Pretending to be evil, as they say that people who love too deeply often do. He wears the garish demon's mask, but that just works against him. It actually weakens his stories. But *East of the River* has this lonesome, immovable strength. I do like it.

The bath is ready. I turn on the light in the bathroom, slip off my kimono, open the window all the way, and sink quietly into the tub. I can see the green leaves of the coral tree outside the window, each individual leaf shining brightly in the glow of the electric light. The stars are twinkling in the sky. No matter how many times

I look up at them, that's what they're doing, twinkling. Lying back dreamily in the tub, I'm vaguely aware of the pale white of my body – I try not to look, but it's there all right, somewhere in my field of vision, and as I lie here I begin to think that my skin is somehow not as fair as it was when I was little. What an unbearable thought. It's so disturbing the way my body goes on changing all by itself, completely independent of my feelings. I can't stand it. It's sad to see myself becoming an adult right before my eyes and knowing I can't do anything about it. Do I just have to resign myself and sit back and watch it happen? I'd like always to have the body of a little girl, a little doll. I splash the bathwater around, as a child might, but somehow it just leaves me feeling dejected. I begin to suffer this sense that I have no real reason to go on living. And then, suddenly, from out in the meadow beyond the garden, I hear a little boy calling for his older sister.

I get all worked up with these thoughts and end up feeling really sorry for myself. Poor, unfortunate little me.

Somehow the stars are weighing on my mind tonight, and after my bath I step out into the garden. It's as if it's raining stars. Ah, summer is near. Frogs are croaking here and there. The barley fields rustle in the breeze. Each time I look up, the stars are there, glittering, lots and lots of them. I think of last year – no, not last year, it's already been two years now. I wanted to go for a walk, and Father, though he was sick, insisted on going with me. My father, youthful to the end. Teaching me a little German ditty that meant something like "Till you are one hundred, and I'm ninety-nine," talking about the stars, improvising poems, leaning on his stick and spitting again and again, blinking the way he did, walking along beside me – my fine, gentle father. I remember him so clearly as I look up at these silent stars. A year, two years have passed since then, and I, little by little, have turned into a naughty girl, a bad girl with lots and lots of secrets she can't tell anyone about.

I go back to my room, sit at the desk with my cheek propped up on my hand, and gaze at the lily before me. It smells so good. With that fragrance in the air, no unclean thoughts or feelings can get to me, even as I sit here alone and bored. I bought the lily yesterday evening, on my way back from taking a walk near the station, and since then it's as if my room is a different room altogether. As soon as you open the door to enter, that fragrance wafts over you, and you feel refreshed and comforted. As I sit here studying this lily, I suddenly recall the saying that Solomon, "even in his glory," was no match for these things, and the truth of it really hits me. I remember last summer in Yamagata. In the mountains there, we saw tons of lilies blooming on the face of a cliff, so many that it was almost otherworldly, and I was spellbound. But the lilies were about halfway up a steep slope that I knew I'd never be able to climb, so I resigned myself to just sighing and taking it all in. But without saying anything, this man who happened to be standing nearby, a young mine worker, started scrambling up the slope and was back before you knew it with so many lilies he could barely hold them in both arms. Then, without so much as a smile, he handed them over to me. I mean, there were just so many of them! I bet no one ever got so many flowers at one time before, not even in the world's most magnificent theater or wedding hall. It was the first time flowers ever made me dizzy. I struggled just to hold that gigantic white bouquet in my arms, and I couldn't see a thing in front of me. I wonder how he's getting along now – that grave and gallant young miner. He picked some flowers for me on a difficult slope. That's all there was to it, but now, whenever I see a lily, I'll always remember him.

I open the desk drawer and start rummaging through it, and there's my fan from last summer. On the white background is a picture of a Genroku-era woman sitting in a slovenly sort of pose, and next to her are two green Chinese lantern plants. Last summer comes wafting up from this fan like smoke. Life in Yamagata, the train, yukata robes, watermelons, rivers, cicadas, wind chimes – all of a sudden I want to take this with me and go board a train. Opening a fan is a nice feeling. The sections say *pop pop pop* as they separate, and then suddenly the fan becomes almost weightless, as if it's floating. I'm still toying with it, twirling it about, when Mother comes home. She's in a good mood.

"Ah, I'm so tired," she grumbles, but she doesn't look all that unhappy about it. It can't be helped – she just loves doing things for people. "Anyway, it's such a complicated affair," she says, going on about the business with the Imaidas as she gets out of her kimono and into the bath.

After her bath, as we're having a cup of tea together, Mother begins to smile at me in a funny way. And what do you suppose she comes out with?

"The other day, didn't you say you were dying to see *Barefoot Girl*? Well, if you want to go so badly, it's all right with me. On one condition: that you massage Mother's shoulders tonight. You'll enjoy the movie even more if you have to work for it, won't you?"

I'm so happy. I *have* been wanting to see that picture, but since I've done nothing but fool around recently, I hesitated to ask Mother to let me go. Obviously she could tell how I felt, though, and by assigning me a task she's giving me a chance to go see a film without feeling guilty. I'm so happy and so full of love for her that I couldn't suppress this smile if I wanted to.

It seems so long since I've last spent time alone with

Mother at night. She has such a busy social life. She too, no doubt, is doing her best not to be made a fool of. Massaging her shoulders like this, I can really feel how tired she is; it's as if her weariness is transmitted right into my own body. I must take good care of her. I'm ashamed of having felt resentment toward her earlier, when the Imaidas were here, and though she can't see me I voicelessly mouth the words "I'm sorry." I'm always so engrossed in myself, always thinking of myself alone, when the only reason I can afford to be so willful is that I trust in Mother's love and protection. But whenever I'm being selfish, I just block out the hurt and pain it causes Mother. She's become so vulnerable since Father passed away. I'm forever clinging to her, saying how hard things are for me, how unbearable it all is; but if she tries to lean on me even a little, I'm repelled, as if she's showing me a filthy side of herself. And that's beyond selfish of me. Both of us are weak women, really. From now on, I want to be content with my life alone with Mother. I always want to know what she's feeling, to talk with her about the past, and about Father, and to set aside a day, even if it's only one day a week, when everything I do centers around her. And I want to feel that I have an admirable, worthwhile life. In my heart, I worry about Mother and tell myself I want to be a good daughter, but all my actions and words are those of a spoiled child. And at this point, nothing remains in me of the purity of childhood. Only unclean, shameful things. *I'm suffering, I'm worried, I'm lonely, I'm sad.* What is it all about? State it clearly, and you die. You know, but you can't say a word – not a single noun or adjective. You just get all flustered and end up losing your temper like ... like I don't know what. They say negative things about women of the olden days – how they were slaves, or puppets, self-effacing nonentities, and so on – but compared to someone like me, they were feminine in the best sense of the word, with huge hearts and the wisdom to handle being submissive without losing their vitality. They knew the beauty of self-sacrifice and the joy of serving others and expecting no compensation.

"My, what a wonderful masseuse you are!" Mother says, teasing me as usual. "You're a genius with those hands."

"It's because I put my heart into it. But you know, Mother, I have other good qualities too. I'd feel awful if all I had going for me was my skill at giving massages. There are other, even better things about me." These words come straight from the heart, which is why I, at least, find them refreshing. I haven't been able to speak my mind so clearly, and so naturally, for the past two or three years.

I'm grateful to Mother for a lot of reasons tonight, and after I've finished the massage, I decide as a bonus to read to her from *Cuore: An Italian Schoolboy's Journal*. She looks relieved to see that I read this kind of book.

A few days ago I was reading Kessel's *Belle de Jour*, and she lifted it out of my hands. Her face clouded over when she looked at the cover, and though she just handed it back without saying anything, I somehow lost interest in reading on. I'm certain that my mother has never heard of *Belle de Jour*, but she intuitively knew what sort of book it is. As I'm reading from *Cuore*, my voice gets unnaturally loud at times, and I feel oddly self-conscious. It's so quiet in the room that the silliness of the prose really stands out. Reading *Cuore* to myself is as moving now as it was when I was little, and it helps me imagine that I've become pure and innocent again. But reading it aloud is completely different. Stunningly different. Still, when I come to the parts about Enrico and Garrone, tears well up in Mother's eyes and she bows her head. My mother, like Enrico's, is a wonderful, beautiful mother.

Mother goes to bed first. She must be awfully tired, having been on the go since early morning. I straighten out the futon for her, patting the edges and fluffing it up. Mother always closes her eyes the moment she gets in bed.

I go back in the bathroom to do the laundry. Lately I've got into this strange habit of doing the laundry when it's nearly midnight. It seems a pity to waste time washing clothes during the day, but maybe I'm the one who's got things backwards. I can see the moon through the window. Squatting down, scrubbing away, I give the moon a little smile. The moon, however, pays no attention to me, and suddenly I have this odd sensation – I'm convinced that at this very same moment, somewhere, some poor, lonely girl is doing her laundry, exactly as I am, and just gave the moon a little smile. I'm certain she exists – some unfortunate, suffering soul, washing clothes at the back door of a house atop a mountain out in the country. And another girl, the same age as I, is alone on the balcony of a run-down apartment on a back street in Paris, doing her laundry, and she, too, just smiled at the moon. There's no doubt in my mind about this. It's as if I'm actually seeing her through a telescope, and even the colors are vivid and clear.

No one really understands how we suffer. One day, when we're adults, we may come to recall this suffering, this misery, as silly and laughable, but how are we to get through the long, hateful period until then? No one bothers to teach us that. Maybe it's like a sickness you just have to wait out, like measles or something. But some people die from measles, and others have had their eyes destroyed by measles. We can't just wait it out. Getting so depressed and angry each day, some among us will eventually make a false step, take a horrible fall, and end up doing irreparable damage to themselves, ruining their whole lives. And some will do away with themselves altogether. When that happens, people will say, "Oh, what a waste! If only she'd lived a bit longer, she'd have understood; as soon as she became a little more mature, she'd have naturally come to understand." But the fact is that from that girl's point of view, she'd suffered and suffered and just barely managed to hold on for that long, always waiting to hear one word from those people but getting nothing but the same evasive platitudes, which are intended to mollify and soothe her but which in fact add up to malignant neglect. By no means are we blind to the future, by no means do we live only for the moment, but to point at some mountain far off in the distance and tell us that everything will be clear once we get to the top of it, that there's a wonderful view up there . . . Well, we know it's exactly as you say; we don't doubt your words for a moment. But what about this fierce misery inside us right now? You just pretend not to notice that. All you have to say is, "There, there, just bear with it a little longer. Once you get to the top of that mountain, you'll have it made." Somebody's mistaken. There's definitely something wrong here. *You*, for instance.

I finish the washing and clean the bathroom, and as soon as I slide open the door to my room, there's that fragrance – the lily. I feel relieved, refreshed. I feel as though my heart has become transparent to the core; I enter a state of what you might call sublime nihilism. I'm quietly changing into my nightgown when Mother, whose eyes are closed and who I thought was fast asleep, surprises me by suddenly speaking. Every now and then she gives me a start like this.

"You were saying you wanted some summer shoes, so when I was in Shibuya today I had a look. Even shoes are expensive these days, aren't they?"

"It's all right. I don't want them so badly anymore."

"But you need them, don't you?"

"Mm."

Tomorrow, no doubt, will be another day just like today. Happiness will never come. I know that. But as you're going to sleep, it's probably better to believe that it will, that it'll be here tomorrow. I collapse on the futon, landing flat and purposely making a loud thump. Ah, it feels good. The padding is cold, and it feels so fresh and cool on my back that I'm immediately, rapturously drowsy. "Happiness comes one night too late." Sleepily I remember those words. Waiting and waiting for happiness, and finally, unable to bear the waiting any longer, leaving home, not knowing that the following day wonderful news will arrive – too late! – to the abandoned house. Happiness . . .

I can hear Kaw out in the garden. *Patter-pat, patter patter-pat*. There's something distinctive about the sound. His right front leg is shorter than the left, and he's severely bowlegged to begin with, and the sound he makes when he's scampering about is so dreary and lonesome. I wonder what he's doing, trotting around in the garden in the middle of the night. Poor Kaw. I was mean to him this morning. Tomorrow I'll give him lots of attention.

I have this sad habit: unless I cover my face with both hands, I can't get to sleep. I cover my face and lie very still.

Falling asleep is a strange sensation. It's as if something heavy hangs by a string from your head, like a big carp or eel at the end of a fishing line, pulling you down. You start to nod off, and then the line goes slack and you jerk back awake. Then it pulls you back down, and again you nod off, and again the line goes slack. That happens three or four times until one great, long tug pulls you under, this time till morning.

Good night. I'm a Cinderella without a prince. You don't know where in Tokyo I am, do you? We won't meet again.

# CHERRY LEAVES
# AND THE WHISTLER

When the blossoms have scattered and new leaves sprout like this on the cherry trees, I always remember that time. It was thirty-five years ago, Father was still alive, and our family (if one can call it that, with Mother having passed away some seven years earlier, when I was thirteen, leaving only Father, my younger sister, and me) lived on the outskirts of a castle town in Shimane Prefecture, a place on the Japan Sea coast with a population of twenty-some thousand. Father had accepted a post as headmaster of a middle school there when I was eighteen and my sister sixteen, but since no suitable lodgings were available in town, we rented two rooms in a detached house on the grounds of a temple near the foot of a mountain, a house we were to live in for six years, until Father was transferred to a middle school in Matsue. I didn't marry until after the move to Matsue, in the autumn of my twenty-fourth year, which in those days was quite late for a girl. With Mother having died so young and Father being so absorbed in his scholarly work and so thoroughly out of touch with worldly matters, I knew that our household would fall apart entirely if I were to leave, and though I'd had a number of offers over the years, I had no desire to be anyone's bride if it meant abandoning my family. Had my sister been healthy, I would have felt somewhat more inclined to do as I pleased, but although she, quite unlike myself, was a lovely and very intelligent child with long, beautiful hair, she was physically infirm, and in the spring of the second year after Father took up that post in the castle town, she died. This is the story of something that happened shortly before her death.

She'd been in a very bad way for quite some time by then. She had renal tuberculosis, a terribly serious disease, and both of her kidneys had been severely damaged before it was detected. The doctor had told Father quite bluntly that the end would come within a hundred days and explained that there was nothing he could do. There was nothing we could do either, of course, but watch in silence as a month passed, another month passed, and even as the hundredth day approached. My sister, not knowing how close to death she was, remained in relatively good spirits, and though she was confined to bed day and night, she cheerfully sang songs and joked and laughed as she let me spoil her, and whenever I reflected that she had only thirty or forty days to live, that this was a medical certainty, it was as if my entire body were being pierced by needles, and I thought I would go mad with the pain. March, April, May ... Yes, it was the middle of May. It's a day I'll never forget.

The meadows and mountains were covered with fresh green, and it had grown warm enough that one almost wanted to shed one's clothing. The new greenery was so brilliant in the sunlight that it stung my eyes as I walked along a meadow path, my head bent and one hand tucked in my sash, turning this and that over in my mind. All my thoughts were so painful that soon I was literally trembling and finding it difficult to breathe. And just then, from deep beneath the verdant earth at my feet, came an eerie, booming, otherworldly sound, faint yet enormous, like giant drums being beaten in hell below, a steady, unbroken rumbling, and I, not knowing what that horrifying sound might be, wondered if I hadn't finally lost my mind. I stood frozen in my tracks until I found myself unable to stand any longer and, with a cry of anguish, collapsed in the long grass and wept and wept.

I later learned that the strange and terrifying sound had, in fact, been the cannon of warships under the command of Admiral Togo, engaged in the battle that was to sink the entire Russian Baltic fleet. And Navy Day is just around the corner again, isn't it? So you see, it was right at that time that all of this happened. In that castle town by the sea everyone must have been in mortal fear, hearing the rumble of those cannon. But I, not knowing what it was and half mad with concern for my sister, believed I was hearing the drums of the netherworld and sat there in the meadow for a very long time, sobbing and afraid even to lift up my eyes. Not until evening began to fall did I stand up at last and walk, in a deathlike trance, back to the temple.

My sister called to me when I got home. She was by now terribly thin and weak, and it seemed that she was beginning to realize she didn't have long to live. She no longer asked me to cater to her whims, to mother and spoil her, and that was only making it all the more painful for me.

"When did this letter come?" she said.

The question gave me such a start, so pierced my breast, that I felt the blood drain from my face.

"When did it come?" she asked again, all innocence.

I pulled myself together and said, "Just awhile ago. While you were sleeping. You were smiling in your sleep. I put it there by your pillow. You didn't notice, did you?"

"No, I didn't." Darkness was falling, and her smile was pale and beautiful in the dim light of the room. "I read the letter, though. It's so strange. I don't know this person."

*Oh, you don't, don't you?* was my unspoken thought. I knew who the sender was: a man who called himself "M.T." Oh, I knew who he was, all right. No, I'd never met him, but five or six days before this I'd been arranging the things in my sister's wardrobe when I came across a bundle of letters tied with a green ribbon and hidden in the bottom of one of the drawers. It wasn't the right thing to do, I suppose, but I untied the ribbon and looked at the letters. There were about thirty of them, and they were all from this Mr. M.T. Mind you, his name and return address weren't written on the envelopes, but all the letters were signed by him; on the envelopes were the names of various girls, all of whom were actual friends of my sister. Father and I never dreamed that she was carrying on such voluminous correspondence with a man.

No doubt this M.T. was a cautious fellow and had asked my sister the names of a number of her friends so that he could write her without arousing suspicion. Having deduced that much, I marveled to myself at the boldness of youth, and it was enough to make me shudder with fear just to imagine what would happen if our stern and severe father were to find out. But when I began reading the final letter, which had been written the previous fall, I suddenly leaped to my feet. The sensation was, perhaps, like being struck by lightning, and I stood bolt upright with the shock. My sister's romance had not been purely platonic – it had progressed to more detestable things.

I burned the letters, every single one. M.T. was, as far

as I could gather, an impoverished poet living in the town – and enough of a coward to have abandoned my sister as soon as he learned of her illness. The cruelest things were written in the final letter, and in the most offhand, breezy way – saying how he and she should try to forget each other, and so on – and since then, apparently, he hadn't written again.

It occurred to me that if I simply kept to myself what I'd just discovered, my sister could remain, to the end, a pure and unsullied young maiden. No one knows, I told myself, and this breast alone shall bear the torment. But learning the truth only made me pity my sister more; I imagined all sorts of outrageous things, and I myself felt a bittersweet sort of ache in my heart, a suffocating, unbearable feeling that no one but a girl coming of age can ever understand. It was a living hell, and I suffered it alone, as if it were *I* who'd had that dreadful experience. I was not quite myself in those days, you see.

"Read it to me, won't you?" she said. "I haven't the slightest idea what it's all about."

Her dishonesty at that moment was repellent to me.

"Are you sure it's all right?" I asked quietly, my fingers trembling in a most discomfiting way as I took the letter. I knew what it said, without opening and reading it. But I had to pretend otherwise. I read it aloud, scarcely looking at the pages.

*Today I must ask your forgiveness. My lack of self-con-fidence is all that has kept me from writing sooner. I am a poor and powerless man. There is nothing I can do to help you. All I have to give you are words. My words contain not the slightest shadow of falsehood, but they are, nonetheless, only words. I began to hate myself for my powerlessness, my inability to offer anything more as evidence of my love for you. I haven't forgotten you for a single moment, not even in my dreams. But I can do noth-ing for you. It was the agony of this realization that made me decide we must part. The greater your misfortune and the deeper my love for you, the more difficult it was for me to approach you. Can you understand that? You mustn't think I'm only making excuses. I believed I was doing the right thing. But I was mistaken. I know now that I was wrong. Forgive me. I only wanted, in my selfishness, to be the ideal man for you. We are solitary, powerless crea-tures, but I now believe that only by sending these faithful and honest, if inadequate, words can I hope to live a life of truth, humility, and beauty. It's not a matter of how great or how insignificant my offering may be. Have I nothing to give you but a single dandelion? Then I shall send it to you, without shame — such, I realize now, is the more courageous, the more manly attitude. I will not run from you again. I love you. Each and every day I shall write you a poem and send it to you. And this too: each*

*and every day I shall stand outside your garden fence
and whistle. I'll be there tomorrow evening at six o'clock,
whistling the "Warship March." I'm a good whistler, you
know. This much, at least, I can easily do. But you mustn't
laugh at me. No, on second thought, please do. Be happy.
God is somewhere, surely, watching over us. I believe that.
You and I are both His children. We're certain to have a
beautiful marriage.*

*I waited and waited
to see them in bloom:
the peach trees this year.
I heard they'd be white;
these flowers are crimson.*

*I'm working hard at my studies. All is going well. Until
tomorrow,*

*— M.T.*

"I know what you did," my sister said in a clear, soft voice.
"Thank you. You wrote this letter, didn't you?"

I was so shocked, so mortified, that I wanted to tear
my hair and rip the letter into a thousand pieces. Distraught – is that the word? I *had* written the letter. I just
couldn't bear to see my sister suffer so, knowing what I
knew, and I intended to write a letter every day, imitating

M.T.'s handwriting, and to include in each one a clumsy attempt at a poem. And, yes, I meant to slip outside the fence each evening at six o'clock and whistle that song for her, until the day she died.

I felt so foolish, having gone so far as to compose bad poetry in my deception, that I was utterly beside myself, unable even to respond.

"You needn't worry." My sister, remarkably calm and composed, gave me an almost sublimely beautiful smile. "You saw the letters tied in that green ribbon, didn't you? They ... they weren't real. You see, I was so lonely that ... Well, a year ago last fall I began writing those letters and sending them to myself. Please don't think me silly. Youth is such a precious thing. I've really come to understand that since I fell ill. I know that writing letters to yourself is pathetic. Perfectly wretched. But I really wish I'd had a chance to do something bold and reckless with a gentleman friend. I would have liked someone to hold me tightly in his arms. Not only have I never had a lover, I've never even talked with a man – outside of our immediate circle, I mean. You haven't either, have you? That was our mistake. We were too sensible. Oh, I hate the thought of dying. My poor hands, my poor fingertips, my poor hair. I don't want to die. I don't!"

I was so sad, and scared, and happy, and ashamed – so full of emotions that I didn't know what I was feeling –

and I put my arms around her and pressed her hollow cheek to mine, my eyes brimming with tears.

And that's when I heard it. It was a faint, soft sound, but there was no mistaking it: someone whistling the "Warship March." My sister heard it too: she turned her head to listen. I looked at the clock, and – ah! – it was just six. Overwhelmed with a nameless dread, we both sat perfectly still, hugging each other tightly, as that uncanny tune continued from beyond the cherry trees in the garden.

There is a God, there really is. I was sure of it then. My sister died three days later. The end came so quietly, and so suddenly, that even the doctor seemed mystified. But it wasn't a shock to me. Everything, I believed, was according to God's will.

Now ... Well, now I'm an old woman with all sorts of shameful, selfish desires. Perhaps my faith isn't as strong as it once was. I've come to wonder if that wasn't my father whistling. He might have returned early from school that day and stood in the next room, listening to us. Pity might have moved him to contrive that little deception – an impetuous act that a staid and serious man like him might perform but once in a lifetime. That's what I sometimes think, but ... No, it's awfully hard to imagine. If Father were still alive, I could ask him, but it's been some fifteen years since he passed away. No, surely it was the work of God.

At least, it would set my heart at ease to believe that. But as I've grown older, I've come to have all these earthly desires, and I know it's a bad thing, but my faith just isn't as strong as it once was.

# SKIN AND SOUL

At the baths I notice a skin eruption, about the size of an azuki bean, under my left breast, and on closer inspection I see that it's surrounded by a spattering of little red specks. It doesn't itch or anything, but I don't like the look of it, so I scrub it vigorously with a washcloth. A mistake, apparently. When I get back home and sit at my dressing table, baring my breast to look in the mirror, I receive a bad shock. It's less than a five-minute walk from the baths to my house, but in that time the outbreak has spread from below my breast to my stomach, forming a strawberry-red patch of skin I can't even cover with both hands. The world goes dark around me, and I feel as if I've been plunged into a vision of Hell. From this moment on, I'm no longer the person I was. In fact, I'm no longer sure I'm a person at all. As I gaze vacantly at myself in the mirror, dark gray thunderheads roll up all around me, and I feel myself being whisked far away from the world I knew. Is this what it means to "swoon"? Familiar sounds grow faint, barely audible, as my relentless slide through this gloomy underworld unfolds. In the mirror, right before my eyes, little specks begin appearing, like the first sprinkles of rain, spreading on my neck, my chest, my stomach, and even along the ribs toward my spine. I reach for a hand mirror, positioning it to show me my back, where more red specks are peppering the pale slope of skin. I bury my face in my hands.

"Look at this rash I got." It's early June, and my husband is sitting at his desk in a short-sleeve shirt and short pants, idly smoking a cigarette, having evidently wrapped up his work for the day. He gets up and walks over to me, then has me turn this way and that, creasing his brow as he peers at the spots, and gently pressing here and there with his fingers.

"Does it itch?" he asks. No, I tell him, I don't feel anything at all. He tilts his head, looking mystified, then leads me to the veranda and has me stand there, naked in the hot afternoon sun. He walks around me slowly, giving every part of me a close inspection. He is, if anything, almost overly solicitous when I experience physical problems, even minor ones. He may not say much, being the taciturn man he is, but he's always very protective of me. Knowing this about him helps me feel at ease, even as he positions me on the veranda in broad daylight, nude and embarrassed, turning me to face east, then west, and lifting my arms and so on, and soon I find myself slipping into a strangely calm, prayerlike state. Standing here with my eyes lightly closed, it occurs to me that I'd just as soon not open them again until my time on earth is over.

"I don't know. If it were hives, it'd be itchy. Couldn't be measles, I don't think."

I manage a pathetic smile and start putting my kimono back on.

"Maybe it's from the rice bran in the soap," I tell him. "Whenever I go to the baths, I scrub my chest and neck and everything really hard, with lots of soap."

His "maybe so" soon turns into "that must be it," and off he goes to the drugstore. He returns with a tube of sticky white medicine, which he wordlessly begins rubbing into the affected areas with his fingertips. I immediately feel a cooling sensation, and a somewhat lightened mood.

"I wonder if it's contagious."

"Don't worry about that."

So he says, but the sadness he feels – which comes, after all, from empathizing with me – is transmitted through his fingertips and reverberates in my troubled breast. My sole desire right now is to lose this abominable rash.

My husband has always refused to admit to any flaws in my decidedly unattractive face. He's never mentioned, even in jest, any of its comically odd features but has in fact looked at me with all the crystal clarity of a blue sky and said:

"I think it's a good face. I like it."

I get flustered and never know how to respond when he says things like this.

Our wedding took place just this past March. I feel a bit pretentious even using the word "wedding" to describe that meager, awkward little ceremony of ours. I'm twenty-eight years old, for starters. Being the homely thing I am, marriage prospects were few, although even I, up to the age of twenty-four or so, had had a few formal arranged meetings, all of which started out promising but soon fell apart. The fact that I hailed from a weakened and by no means wealthy family consisting of only three women – my mother, my sister, and I – did not help my chances, and I had no real hope for a good match. Marriage was only a dream, driven I suppose by unfathomable desire. When I turned twenty-five, I vowed to myself that even if I never married, I would continue to assist my mother and help raise my little sister, and that this would serve as my life's purpose. My sister is seven years younger, twenty-one this year. She has nice features, and she's developing an excellent character now that she's outgrown the selfishness of childhood. We needed to find a good husband for her, an adopted son-in-law for Mother, before

I tried to make a life on my own. Until then, I decided, I would continue overseeing everything, from the family finances to our social activities, with the intention of protecting our home. Once I'd made this decision, all the worries I'd been holding inside evaporated, and all the pain and loneliness went away too. In addition to taking care of household affairs, I was earnestly learning the art of dressmaking. When one neighbor, and then another, asked me to make clothing for their children, I began to see this as a potential means of supporting myself in the future. And it was just at this time that an arranged meeting with the man who is now my husband was first proposed. The gentleman who brought us this proposal had been a benefactor of my father's, and we therefore owed him a debt of gratitude and couldn't just flatly refuse. Looking into the details, we discovered that the man's education had ended after primary school, and that he had no parents or siblings. He'd been supported by my father's benefactor since childhood and naturally had no fortune or assets of his own. He was thirty-five. He was a rather accomplished graphic designer, whose monthly earnings averaged about seventy or eighty yen – sometimes more than two hundred but at other times zero. Furthermore, this wouldn't be his first marriage; he had lived for six years with a woman he loved but for some reason had parted with her the year before last, after which, having little education and no assets to speak of, and being no longer young, he couldn't expect to find a proper marriage partner and was resigned to spending the rest of his life as an unattached bachelor. That's when Father's benefactor had a talk with him, saying that the world would treat him as an oddball if he lived alone as a divorced man, and since nothing good could come of that, he should hurry up and find himself a bride, and it so happened that he, the benefactor, already had someone in mind. When the proposal was brought to us confidentially, my mother and I exchanged troubled looks. There was nothing appealing about the offer. Though I was an old maid, and homely to boot, I was chaste and unsullied. To think that if I wanted to marry, a man like this was the best I could do, made me angry at first, and then indescribably sad. I had no choice but to decline the offer, but we couldn't ignore our debt of gratitude to the man who brought it to us. Mother and I agreed that it was best to take our time in refusing, rather than giving a quick and definitive no, but as we procrastinated, I began to feel sorry for the man. He was probably a very gentle person. I myself had only graduated girls' school and was far from being the scholarly type. Nor did I have much of a dowry to speak of. Father was gone, and we were a weakened household. And I, as you can see, was a homely person and no longer young. It was actually *my* side that had nothing much to offer. Maybe we were a perfect match. After all, I was already unhappy. Rather than decline and make things awkward with my late father's benefactor ... Such was my line of thought as my feelings began to bend his way and, embarrassingly enough, there were times when a blushingly buoyant mood would come over me. "Are you sure you're all right with this?" Mother would ask, with a worried look on her face. Eventually I decided to stop discussing it with her and went directly to my late father's benefactor, to accept the proposal in person.

After the wedding, I was happy. No, honestly, I have to say I was happy; heaven might strike me down if I claimed otherwise. I was exceedingly well cared for. The man is timid by nature and had probably been made even more so by having been dumped, which is apparently what had happened. He lacked confidence to an exasperating degree. He's small and thin, with a sickly-looking face. But he's extremely diligent when it comes to his work. The first time he showed me some of his designs, I spotted one that I knew very well indeed. What an incredible coincidence! When he confirmed that the design was his, my heart went all aflutter for the first time, as if I was actually falling in love. This man hadn't only designed the "rambling rose" logo of the famous cosmetics emporium in Giza but labels for their perfume, soap, face powder, and so on, as well as most of their newspaper advertisements. He said he'd begun working exclusively for the cosmetics firm some ten years ago and had created and drawn the rambling rose designs basically all on his own. Even people who couldn't tell you the name of the firm have seen and remember that design, with its sinuous, gracefully entwined rose canes, and now it's recognized even overseas. I'd been familiar with that logo from the time I was in girls' school. I was strangely drawn to the design, and once I'd finished school I used the products of that cosmetics firm exclusively; I was, so to speak, a fan. But I never once wondered about the designer of the rambling rose. Rather thoughtless of me, I suppose, but I'm not the only one: nobody who looks at those beautiful newspaper layouts, for example, ever wonders who the designer is. He's like a shadow warrior, an unsung hero. I'd been married to the man for some time by then but hadn't even known about all this. The discovery thrilled me.

"I've loved this design since I was in school. So, you're the one who created it? Oh, that makes me so happy! It means I've had a mysterious connection with you for, what, ten years? I guess it was my destiny to be with you." I was acting rather giddy, I suppose. His face reddened.

"Don't be ridiculous." He winced, blinking rapidly. "It's just a work of manual labor," he said, and gave a short, mirthless laugh.

The man is forever belittling himself. He bemoans his

lack of education, the fact that he was previously married, his "rodent-like" looks, and so on – things that don't even bother me. How is a homely, former old maid supposed to respond to such self-deprecation? Both husband and wife are insecure, lacking confidence, and both have wrinkles of worry and shame etched into their faces. At times he seems to want me to baby him, but I myself am an old woman of twenty-eight years, and an ugly one to boot. What's more, his self-deprecating tendencies have clearly rubbed off on me, exacerbating my awkwardness, so that I'm not capable of simply and naturally displaying affection. My heart longs to do so, but instead I respond with a kind of solemn frigidity, which in turn sours his mood, further contributing to the tension I feel, and I end up relating to him as if we were strangers. He does seem to understand my own lack of confidence, however, and once in a while, out of the blue, he'll clumsily compliment something about me – my hair, for example, or the pattern on my kimono. I know it's only his way of trying to be supportive, but his inept attempts at flattery never make me the least bit happy; they only bring pain to my heart and tears to my eyes. He's a good person, though. He's never made so much as the slightest allusion to his first wife, thanks to which I don't have to ruminate on all that. We rented this house in Tsukiji after our marriage. Before that he had lived alone in an apartment in

Akasaka, and when we moved here, he brought only his
work tools, having sold off all his furniture and household
accessories – partly, I'm sure, to avoid evoking memories
of the bad times but also, I believe, out of kind consideration for my feelings. I, for my part, brought a modest
sum of money my mother gave me, as well as a futon and
a chest of drawers from my home in Hongo, and together
we bought the things we needed for the household, little
by little. Not so much as a whiff of the previous woman
remains, and at this point I can scarcely believe that he
spent six whole years with someone else. If only he didn't
have that unwarranted low self-esteem and was a little
more rough around the edges, at least occasionally yelling
at me and being more domineering, I believe I could be
content just to hum little songs and bask in his embrace,
completely dependent on his protection. It would bring a
lot of sunshine to this little house. But we're both keenly
aware of our own undesirability, as a result of which we
still feel ill at ease with each other. Leaving aside my
own case, why would the man think so little of himself?
Though he graduated only primary school, in terms of
cultural sophistication he's on a level with any Bachelor
of Arts. His collection of phonograph records displays ex-
quisite taste; he reads voraciously between assignments,
including recent works by foreign authors I've never even
heard of; and he is the man, lest we forget, who came up

with that world-famous rambling rose design. He often mocks his own poverty, but recently he's had a number of assignments, from which sizable cash payments come in (a hundred yen here, two hundred yen there), such that he was able to take me to a hot springs resort in Izu not long ago. And yet it bothers him to this day that the futon and dresser and a few other items in our house were purchased by my mother, and the fact that it bothers him makes it all the more awkward for me; I feel as if I've done something wrong. They're all just cheap things anyway, and the whole issue is ridiculous, but it makes me so miserable I could cry. There have even been nights when I've fallen prey to horrible thoughts (*it's a mistake to marry out of compassion or pity; maybe I'd have been better off alone*), and a detestable, unchaste desire for someone stronger has even reared its head. I'm a bad person. Only after marrying did I begin to feel a heart-wrenching regret for having wasted the beauty of youth in a gray, bleak world. I wanted somehow to make up for that now, with him, and one night, sitting quietly together at dinner, I couldn't take the loneliness any longer and with my chopsticks and rice bowl still in hand, I burst into tears. It's all about my own frustrated desires, I know. And it makes me a worthy target of mockery – the homely one talking about lost youth, what a joke. And the truth is that right now I have more happiness than I deserve. I mustn't think otherwise. I heedlessly allowed my selfishness to emerge, and because of that I've been cursed with this infernal skin rash. It has stopped spreading, perhaps because of the ointment my husband applied, and maybe it will all be gone tomorrow. I inwardly pray to God that it will be so, as I excuse myself and retire, earlier than usual.

Lying here in bed, my mind racing, I end up marveling at this situation. I've never feared illness, with the singular exception of skin disease. I've always believed I could bear any degree of poverty or suffering, as long as it wasn't something like this. I thought I would much rather lose a leg or an arm than contract a serious skin condition. In physiology class at girls' school, when we learned about pathogens that cause skin problems, it made me feel itchy all over. The textbook had photos and illustrations of the bugs and bacteria responsible, and I wanted to rip those pages out and tear them to shreds. And the teacher's insensitivity to all this was abominable to me. Well, he probably wasn't actually indifferent to it but had to squelch his disgust in order to fulfill his professional duties, but that didn't make his brazenness any less despicable to me. I writhed in discomfort, and when that lesson ended I found myself getting into a debate with classmates. To be in pain, to be tickled, or to itch – which of these three is the worst? That was the subject of our debate, and I insisted that itchiness was clearly the most dreadful. I mean, think about it. The sensations of being in pain or of being tickled are limited by nature. I'm sure that once the agony of being beaten or stabbed, or even tickled, reaches a certain extremity, the victim will lose consciousness. Once you pass out, you're in dreamland. You ascend to heaven and cleanly escape all suffering. And if you die, that's all right too. But itchiness comes in waves that rise and fall, surge and recede, in an endless, slow slither, squirming and wriggling all over you, but in the end the agony never quite reaches a climax, so you can't even faint, and I'm pretty sure you can't die of itching either, meaning that you're stuck with this lukewarm misery that just leaves you squirming. No, when it comes to suffering, nothing tops itchiness.

If I were tortured by authorities back in the Edo period, they could cut me, hit me, tickle me mercilessly, but I would never confess. What's the worst that could happen? I'd pass out two or three times and then die. Confess? Me? I would put my life on the line to protect my comrades. But what would happen if you brought a bamboo flask full of fleas, lice, and those tiny scabies bugs and told me you were going to dump it all down my back? Every hair on my body would stand on end, and I'd wobble with fear, clasp my hands in supplication, and squeal, "I'll tell you everything! Have mercy on me!" So much for being a heroine. Just thinking about such torture is enough to make me flinch and quiver. I expressed this during our little impromptu debate, and all the others instinctively shrieked their agreement. One time, the teacher took our entire class to the Museum of Nature and Science in Ueno, and I believe it was in the specimen room on the third floor that I inadvertently let out a scream and ended up crouched on the floor, bawling bitterly. I had just seen sculpted models of a variety of skin parasites, magnified to the size of crabs, displayed shoulder to shoulder in a long glass case. "Dammit!" I shouted, so angry that I wanted to take a bludgeon and pound all those models to dust. For the next three days, I had trouble sleeping, felt vaguely itchy, and didn't have any appetite. I don't even like chrysanthemums. The way those creepy little petals wriggle around reminds me of something. When I look at the rough bumps on tree bark, it makes me shiver and feel itchy all over. Salted salmon roe – how do people eat something that looks like that? Oyster shells. Pumpkin rinds. Gravel paths. Insect-eaten leaves. Cockscombs. Sesame seeds. Shibori dyed cloth. Used tea leaves. Shrimp. Beehives. Strawberries. Ants. Lotus nuts. Fish scales. These are all things I hate. Fine print too – the tiny phonetic notations next to some words look like lice to me. Silverberries, mulberries, I don't like either one. I once nearly vomited after seeing a close-up photograph of the moon. As for embroidery, it depends on the design, but most of it I can't stand. Naturally, having such an extreme aversion to diseases of this sort, I've always taken great care to protect my skin and until now have never experienced a serious problem of any sort. Since marrying, I go to the baths every day and scrub every inch of myself with rice-bran soap. That might have been the problem; maybe I scrubbed too hard. Having my skin erupt like this is a bitter pill, especially vexing for me. What sort of horrible thing have I done to deserve this? God has gone too far this time. It's not as if there aren't any number of illnesses He might have chosen; the thing I dreaded most has happened to me. It's like hitting the little golden bullseye with one shot, dropping me straight into the pit I fear most. It's just baffling to me how this could happen.

The next morning I awaken at first light and go straight to my dressing table to face the mirror, only to moan: *Oh no . . .* I'm a goblin. This is not me. It's as if my entire body has been rubbed down with ripe, seed-filled tomatoes. On my neck and chest, and on my stomach, are these hideous bean-size eruptions that cover the skin and make it look as if I'm growing a thousand tiny horns, or sprouting mushrooms, and it has now spread to both legs. It's so far beyond the pale that part of me just wants to laugh hysterically. Ogre. Demon. I'm not a human being. Let me just die like this. I mustn't weep. Imagine this monster on the verge of tears: there would be nothing endearing about it. Comical, shameful, hopeless, and tragic, yes; endearing, no. So, no tears. Cover up. He doesn't know yet. I wish I could keep it that way. Ugly to begin with, and now covered with this festering mess, I have no redeeming features at all. I'm trash. Garbage. When he sees me like this, not even he will find any words to console me. Not that I want to be consoled. If he even tries to console me after seeing me like this, I'll have nothing but contempt for him. I'd even consider leaving him. He mustn't take pity on me. He mustn't look at me. He shouldn't even be near me. I need a much bigger house. I want to spend the rest of my life in a room far away from everyone else. I should never have married. I wish I hadn't lived to the age of twenty-eight. In the winter of my nineteenth year, when I came down with pneumonia, I wish I hadn't recovered but rather had given up the ghost. If I had died then, I wouldn't have to experience this excruciating, shameful, unsightly, miserable state. With my eyes tightly closed, sitting perfectly still but breathing heavily, I begin to feel as if my heart is hardening; a hush falls over the world, and I know I'm no longer the person I was until yesterday. The beast gets up and climbs into her kimono. Thank goodness for clothing. A kimono hides even the most hideous body. Spurring myself on, I go outside, step up onto the clothes-drying platform, and peer sternly at the rising sun, inadvertently breathing a deep sigh. I can hear someone's radio blaring the commands for morning calisthenics. I try a few tentative moves all alone, counting along with the announcer under my breath and trying to lift my spirits, but then, all at once, I see myself as hideously pathetic and can't go on with the exercises. I feel tears welling up, and, perhaps because of the sudden vigorous movements, I feel a dull pain in my neck and underarms and lymph glands. I softly touch these spots and find that all of them are swollen and hard. My knees buckle at this discovery, and I collapse and plop down in a sitting position. Being so unattractive, I've always been a reserved, retiring person, preferring to remain in the background, never wanting to stand out. What have I done to be tormented like this? Boiling over with a red-hot, implacable rage, I inwardly shout this question to no one in particular; and just then, from behind me:

"Oh, *here* you are." He lightly rests a hand on my shoulder. "You mustn't let it get you down, you know," he murmurs. "Is it any better?"

I mean to say yes, it is, but as I stand up, letting his hand slip from my shoulder, the words "I'm going back home to Mother" come out of my mouth. I don't understand myself, and I can't take responsibility for anything I do or say, since I no longer trust myself, or the universe, or anything.

"Let me see." His voice is muffled, as if reaching me from a distance, and he sounds confused.

"No." I pull away. "Now I've got lumps." I touch my underarms. "Here." And then I burst into tears, really letting myself go, sobbing uncontrollably. It's disgraceful. A homely twenty-eight-year-old woman crying for sympathy – there's nothing sweet or charming about that. I know I'm making a ludicrous scene, but the tears just keep coming, along with a lot of sniveling and even dribbling. There's just nothing about me that's of any use at all.

"All right, stop crying!" His voice resonates with a strength and resolution I've never heard from him before. "I'm taking you to see a doctor."

Declaring a day off from his work, he begins scouring the newspaper ads. He decides on a dermatologist whose name even I have heard once or twice. As I'm changing into my better kimono, I ask my husband if he thinks I'll have to show the doctor my entire body.

"Of course." He smiles in a knowing, sophisticated way. "We don't want him mistaking you for a man."

I feel my face reddening, along with a faint flush of happiness.

When we step outside, the sun is blindingly bright, and I see myself as something like a particularly hideous caterpillar. I wish the whole world would turn black as night, at least until I'm cured of this curse.

"Not the train." This is the first time in our marriage that I've demanded any kind of selfish luxury. But the rash has spread as far as the backs of my hands. I remember once seeing a woman on the train with horrifying hands like this. It made me hesitant even to touch the hand straps for fear of catching something, and now I was that woman, with the same frightful hands. The vulgar expression "dealt a bad hand" never cut me to the bone before, as just the thought of it does now.

"I know," he says, with an optimistic look on his face, and hails a taxi. From Tsukiji to the hospital, behind the Takashima-ya department store in Nihonbashi, is a fairly short trip, but I feel as if I'm riding in a funeral hearse the entire way. Only my eyes are alive, gazing out at the early summer fashions of women and men on the street, and I'm dumbfounded to think that nobody else out there is suffering a rash like mine.

At the hospital, he and I enter the waiting room, an entirely different world. I'm reminded of the mise-en-scène of a play I saw at a little theater in Tsukiji long ago called *The Lower Depths*. Outside the windows, the scenery is deep green and the sunshine is almost blindingly bright, but somehow the light is dim in here, and the air is chilly and moist, with a sour smell that stings the nostrils. The place is packed with blind people, sitting or milling about with bowed heads. Most of them aren't really blind of course, but many seem disabled, and I'm surprised by the number of very old people. I sit down on the edge of a bench near the entrance and slump there with my eyes shut, as if dead. It occurs to me that of all these patients, I might be the one with the worst skin condition. The thought is daunting, and I open my eyes and lift my head to study each of the others surreptitiously. Sure enough, no one seems to be suffering a skin rash like mine. From a sign at the entrance to the clinic I learned that this place specializes in two separate categories of pathology – skin diseases and another, even more disturbing class of illnesses that I would rather not name. The handsome young man sitting over there, who looks like a movie star, has no visible rash, so he's probably not here for his skin but the other thing. And once that thought occurs to me I begin to wonder if that isn't what all the slouching, corpse-like patients in this waiting room are suffering from.

"Why don't you go for a walk or something?" I suggest. "This place is depressing."

"It's going to be quite a while yet, I guess," he says. He's standing next to me with nothing to do.

"Yes. They said it probably won't be my turn until noon or so. It's unpleasant in here. You really shouldn't stay." The sternness in my voice surprises me, but he seems to accept my advice and nods.

"Don't you want to come with me?"

"No. I'll be fine." I smile at him. "I'm more at ease here than I would be anywhere else."

After escorting him out of the waiting room, I feel a bit more relaxed. I sit back down on the bench and close my eyes, scrunching them tight, as if I'm biting into a lemon. I'm sure I look absurdly affected to others, a middle-aged lady putting on airs, deeply contemplating stupid things. But this is how I'm most comfortable. I tell myself I'm "playing possum," a phrase I've always found amusing. But I'm starting to worry again. *Everyone has secrets.* It's as if these unpleasant words are whispered into my ear, and something trembles inside me. *Maybe even this rash* ... Every hair on my body stands on end at the emerging thought. Is it possible that this outbreak is somehow a reaction to his gentleness and diffidence? Of course not. But right now, for the first time – it's strange, but for the very first time – the fact that he was previously married hits home, and all of a sudden I'm beside myself. I was deceived! Marriage fraud! These and other, more unsavory accusations flash through my mind. I want to run out after him, grab him, and slap his face. Oh, what a fool I am. I knew everything from the start and still chose to move in with this man; and now I'm left, suddenly, with a bitter, implacable rage. I feel doomed. The mere thought of his previous wife is like the weight of the world on my chest, and for the first time I fear and hate her. It brings tears to my eyes to think that I've been so oblivious all this time. It's physically painful; is this what they call jealousy? If so, jealousy is a madness of the flesh, with no way out. It's a dark and hideous thing, without an iota of beauty about it. I guess this world contains deeper levels of hell than I ever expected. I've grown so tired of living, I think; and, ashamed of myself for that thought, I quickly undo the furoshiki bundle on my lap to pull out my novel. I flip it open to any old page and begin reading at random. *Madame Bovary*. Emma's suffering-filled life is always a consolation for me. And I always end up feeling that the road to her fall is the most natural, the most womanly path for her to take. There's a languid sort of docility about her, like water passively flowing to lower levels. That's what a woman is. She has secrets she can never reveal, a trait innate to all women, though each has her own dark quagmire to deal with. This I can state unequivocally. In the end, for a woman, today is everything. It's not like that for men. Women don't contemplate death or the afterlife. We don't speculate about such things. Moment by moment we seek only the perfection of beauty. We adore life, the *feel* of life. A woman loves fine teacups and pretty designs on kimonos and so on because such things are what she inherently lives for. Each movement, from moment to moment, is itself her life's purpose. She needs nothing more. If your noble realism were to mercilessly expose women's insolence and faithlessness, how much easier would it be for all of us to correct such things? But no one touches on the ever-thirsty "demon" that possesses a woman. Everyone pretends, rather, not to notice it, which causes all manner of tragedies. It may be that only your lofty and profound realism can really save us, but the truth about a woman's heart is this: even on the day after her wedding, she can daydream about another man and think nothing of it. Never put your faith in the human heart.

Suddenly the old saw that "after age seven, boys and girls should be kept apart" strikes me with all the fearsome power of naked reality. Japanese logic is based on the hard realism of brute strength, and it's shockingly disorienting to come to that realization. All is revealed. That this murky territory was mapped out long ago is conversely a rather refreshing and comforting thought. Even with an unsightly, rash-covered body, I'm still a bawdy old broad, I tell myself, and have to smile at this sad joke as I begin reading again. Rodolphe has just pulled Emma closer and is whispering rapid-fire sweet nothings in her ear. As I read, I'm thinking about something completely different and find myself grinning. What if Emma had been suffering at that moment from an outbreak like mine? This peculiar thought strikes me as funny but also as an important question. Emma would have undoubtedly resisted Rodolphe's seduction in that case. And her entire life would have turned out differently. There's no question about it. She would have rejected him no matter what he said or did. I mean, she could not have done otherwise. Not with a body like that. But it would have been a tragedy nonetheless. A woman's life is determined by minutiae – her hairdo, the pattern on her kimono, sleepiness, minor health issues, any one of a thousand things. One woman was so sleep-deprived that she famously murdered the bawling baby on her back by wringing its neck. There's no telling how drastically a skin disease could overturn a woman's fate and disrupt her romantic life. If on the night before her long-awaited marriage, a rash like this were to appear unexpectedly on a woman and rapidly spread all over her torso and limbs, what could she do? Ordinary precautions can't protect you from a skin disease. It would seem to be a question of divine will; or should I say divine *ill* will? A young bride who's gone to the pier in Yokohama to greet her husband on his return from Korea after five years, her heart dancing with anticipation, finds that a purple boil has appeared prominently on her face, and as she probes it with her fingertips, she finds herself turning into something like the poisoned ghost Oiwa-sama, her face erupting, too ugly to look at twice. A tragedy like this is all too possible. Men are apparently untroubled by skin eruptions, but a woman's skin is her very life. Any woman who says that isn't so, is a liar. I don't know much about Flaubert, but he seems to have been fastidious in his realism. When Charles tries to kiss Emma's shoulder she stops him, saying, "Don't! You'll wrinkle my dress." Such an eye for detail. So why didn't Flaubert ever write about the suffering of a woman with skin disease? Maybe men can't understand this sort of misery. Or perhaps a man of Flaubert's genius understood well enough but shied away from such an unclean subject, deeming it improper for a fictional romance. But to shy away from something that's real is sneaky and dishonest. If I unexpectedly came down with this horrific rash the night before my wedding, or just as I was waiting to see my beloved for the first time in five years, I'd just die. I'd run away and fall as low as a woman can go, and then I'd kill myself. A woman lives only for the joy of beauty from moment to moment. Whatever might happen tomorrow –

The door opens quietly, and he pokes his squirrel-like face inside and asks me with his eyebrows: *Not yet?* I beckon to him with an inelegant flapping of my hand.

"Listen!" I've built up steam in this vulgar train of thought, and my voice comes out so loud and shrill that I startle myself. I sink back in my seat and begin again, all but whispering. "Listen. When a woman convinces herself that it doesn't matter what may come tomorrow, that's when she's at her most womanly. Don't you agree?"

"What's that again?" He looks confused. I chuckle to myself.

"I'm so bad with words, no wonder you don't understand. But never mind. Sitting here all this time, I began to feel as if, I don't know, as if I've undergone another complete transformation. It's not good, hitting rock bottom like this. I'm a weak person, easily influenced by the atmosphere around me. I just go along. And that's made me more common, more coarse. My heart is in tatters, and I see myself falling, like a – " I clamp my mouth shut. I was going to say "prostitute," a word no woman should ever pronounce. It's a word that, once uttered, is a source of endless torment. Whenever a woman has lost all pride, she will think of this. This rash has turned even my heart to stone, I reflect, beginning to dimly understand the reality of my situation. I've always described myself as homely, so homely, pretending to have no self-confidence whatsoever, but now I realize that I've always secretly cherished and taken pride in this one feature – my lovely skin. The pride I always took in my humility, my modesty and submissiveness, was a sham and not to be trusted. The truth, as I see it now, is that I've always been a pathetic woman, going through life like a blind person whose ups and downs are dictated by my own perceptions and impressions. However acute my perceptions and impressions might be, these are animalistic faculties and have nothing to do with intelligence. It's abundantly clear to me now that I'm nothing but a dimwitted idiot.

I was mistaken. I considered the delicacy of my perceptions something noble and refined while mistaking it for intelligence. Wasn't this simply a way of consoling myself? The reality is that I'm a foolish, ignorant person.

"I've been thinking about all kinds of things. I'm an idiot. I completely lost my mind."

"I don't blame you. Completely understandable," he says, with a sagacious smile, and I get the sense that he really does understand. "Oh! It's our turn."

A nurse leads us into a consultation room, and I undo my obi sash and bare my skin for the doctor to see. I glance at my breasts and see two red pomegranates. The doctor sits facing me, but knowing that the nurse behind me can see my skin is many times more distressing. The doctor, after all, is not just another person. And he doesn't treat me as a person either but as a subject, or maybe an object. His facial expression tells me nothing as he pokes and pinches my skin here and there.

"It's food poisoning," he says calmly. "You must have eaten something that had gone bad."

"Can it be cured?" my husband asks.

"Absolutely."

I listen vacantly, feeling as if I'm not even in the room.

"She's been crying her eyes out. It's hard to watch."

"We'll give her an injection. She'll be better in no time."

The doctor stands up.

"So, it's a simple thing to fix?"

"It is, yes."

I get my shot, and we leave the clinic.

"Look. My hands are better already."

I hold them up in the sunlight and gaze at them again and again as we walk.

"Are you happy now?"

I'm so embarrassed when he asks me this.

# NO ONE KNOWS

No one knows about this (Mrs. Yasui began with a chuckle), but something very strange once happened to me. It was the spring of my twenty-third year, nearly twenty years ago now, just before the Great Kanto earthquake. This part of Ushigome hasn't changed much since then. The street out front has been widened a bit, eating up half of our garden, and the pond we used to have was filled in as well, but other than that, not much is different. From the upstairs balcony you can still see Mount Fuji, and we can still hear the bugles at the Imperial Army training grounds each morning and evening.

Father was a governor in Nagasaki Prefecture before he was offered the position of mayor here. That was in the summer of my twelfth year, when Mother was still alive. Father was born in Tokyo, right here in Ushigome, but my grandfather was from Morioka. Grandfather drifted to Tokyo alone as a young man and forged a somewhat dodgy career as what was called a "gentleman broker" – half politician and half businessman – and acquired considerable wealth and success. He was barely middle-aged when he purchased this house in Ushigome and retired to a life of ease. I don't know if it's true or not, but it's said that he grew up in the same hometown as Hara Takashi, who was famously assassinated in Tokyo Station all those years later. Grandfather was his senior in terms of both age and political experience and actually gave orders to Hara, who later on, even after becoming a cabinet minister, would apparently call at this house in Ushigome to pay his respects every New Year's, but, again, I'm not sure how much of that is to be believed. Grandfather himself related it all to me when I was twelve and arrived at this house with my parents on their return to Tokyo. Until then, Grandfather had been living here alone, and now he was a slovenly old man in his eighties. I, for my part, had already lived in various places, as my father, a government official, was transferred from Urawa to Kobe to Wakayama to Nagasaki. I was born in a government residence in Urawa and had visited the house here in Tokyo only a handful of times, so I wasn't very familiar with Grandfather. At twelve, when I first settled in here, he felt like a stranger to me, an ugly and repulsive old man. He also spoke with a strong, almost indecipherable northern accent, which didn't help endear him to me. I just didn't take to him at all, and he tried everything he could think of to get on my good side. He told me the Hara Takashi story one summer night on the veranda overlooking the garden, where he sat with legs crossed, fanning himself like this, elbow on knee. I soon grew bored and yawned, but he happened to notice this out of the corner of his eye and immediately changed the subject. "No interest in Hara Takashi, got it. How about the Seven Wonders of Ushigome? Long, long ago ..." And so on, narrating a spooky tale in a whisper. There was something devious about the old man, and in my opinion the Hara Takashi story couldn't be taken at face value. When I asked Father about it later, he smiled in a wistful way, patted my head, and gently informed me that Hara may indeed have visited this house once or so, and that Grandfather doesn't tell lies. Grandfather passed away when I was sixteen. I had never liked him, but I cried a lot at his funeral. Maybe it was the grandeur and magnificence of the ceremony that got to me. The following day, in school, all the teachers I saw offered me their condolences, and I wept every time. Even my classmates were surprisingly sympathetic.

I was born when my father was forty and serving as director of school affairs in Urawa. I was the first and only child, and both Mother and Father, as well as other relatives and family friends, treated me like a princess. I nonetheless considered myself an unfortunate girl, shy and lonely, but looking back on it now, I can see that I was a terribly spoiled and haughty child.

Soon after entering the girls' school in Ichigaya, I made friends with a classmate named Serikawa-san, and although at the time I believed I was a kind and thoughtful friend to her, again, thinking back on it now, I have to wonder. I was terribly stuck up in those days, and an impartial observer might have judged my attitude as being one of reluctantly condescending to be nice to an inferior. Serikawa-san, for her part, was docile enough to go along with everything I said, so that our relationship took on a bit of a master-and-servant flavor. Serikawa-san's house was just across from ours, and – you remember Kazuki-Do, the confectioner's? Yes, it's still there, as prosperous as ever and still featuring those famous chestnut bean-jam cakes. Well, that's her family's shop. The next generation has taken over the business now, and Serikawa-san's elder brother heads the family. He's at the shop every day from early morning to late evening, giving it his all, and his wife too is a diligent sort, always at the reception desk taking orders by telephone and dispatching the delivery boys. Three years after graduating from girls' school, my friend Serikawa-san managed to marry a good man. I haven't seen her for almost twenty years now, but apparently the two of them are living in Keijo, the capital of Korea. Her husband is a handsome devil who graduated from a private school in Mita, and I hear that he manages the Something-or-Other Daily, a big newspaper firm in Keijo.

Serikawa-san and I maintained our friendship after graduating, but never once did I visit her at her house; she always came to mine, and our conversations were usually about works of fiction. She had been an avid reader of authors like Soseki and Roka when we were in school, and her essays and compositions were always very mature and well written, whereas I was completely useless when it came to that sort of thing. It simply didn't interest me at all. Nonetheless, after graduation, I would sometimes pick up one of the novels Serikawa-san brought me and while away an hour or two reading, and in the course of doing so I began to see, to some extent, what people find so interesting about novels. But the books I enjoyed most were ones she never considered particularly good; whereas the books she did consider good, I couldn't even understand very well. I liked Ogai's historical stories, but Serikawa-san laughed at me for that and called me old-fashioned. She told me that Arishima Takeo was a much more serious and important writer, and she lent me two or three of his books, but I had no idea what the man was going on about. If I were to read his work now, I might feel differently about it; but at the time, this Arishima fellow struck me as a bore, with all his convoluted arguments about things that don't matter one way or the other. I guess I was always something of a lowbrow. Among the many up-and-coming young novelists of the time were such writers as Mushanokoji and Shiga, as well as Tanizaki Junichiro, Kikuchi Kan, Akutagawa. Of these, I liked the short stories of Shiga Nagoya and Kikuchi Kan best, but again Serikawa-san laughed at me and said something about my ideology being underdeveloped. I had no use for works that were loaded with theories and logic, however. Whenever Serikawa-san came to visit, she would bring the latest magazines and story collections and enthusiastically explain the different plotlines or gossip about the authors. I thought it a little odd that she got so excited about such things, until the day I discovered the probable source of all this passion.

Women, once they become friends, tend to show one another their photograph albums. Serikawa-san brought hers, a big fat one, to my house one day. As I studied one photo after another, half listening to her somewhat overly thorough explanations, we came to a picture of a very handsome student standing in front of a rose garden with a book in his hand. "That person's awfully good looking, isn't he?" I blurted out, my cheeks growing warm for some reason, but Serikawa-san gave a little cry and snatched the album from my hands. *Aha!* was my immediate thought, but I maintained my composure and simply said, "It's all right. I already saw him." Serikawa-san's face lit up with a big smile. "You can tell?" she said. "Really? I can't put anything past you, can I. Did you know right away? It's been going on since girls' school. You knew all along, didn't you?" She went on, speaking rapidly, giddily, and though I hadn't known about any of this until that moment, she told me everything. She was truly an open and innocent person. The handsome student in the photo and Serikawa-san had met through the readers' column, or whatever it's called, of a literary magazine – where readers can write in and discuss things with others? The two of them wrote a few messages back and forth and "resonated" with each other, as she put it, though I'm not sophisticated enough to understand exactly what it meant. From there they started corresponding directly, and after graduation their feelings quickly intensified, and they decided to marry. She told me that he was the second son of the owner of a shipbuilding firm in Yokohama and an outstanding student at Keio University, that he was on track to become a successful author, and many other details, but it all struck me as horrifying, and even a tad repulsive. At the same time, envy clouded my pounding heart, though I tried not to let it show on my face. "That's great," I told her. "Just be careful."

Serikawa-san could see through my mask, however, and took offense. "You're mean," she said. "Always ready to unsheathe your hidden dagger. Always looking down on me, as coldly as if you were Diana herself." It wasn't like her to attack me so spiritedly, and I immediately apologized. "I'm sorry. I don't look down on you. If I seem cold, please understand that it's just . . . an unfortunate flaw of mine, something in my personality that people take the wrong way, but the truth is, I'm frightened for both of you. He's too handsome. Maybe I'm just envious, but . . ." I was confessing my true thoughts, and Serikawa-san's mood brightened in response. "There you go," she said. "The only one in my family I've told is my big brother, and he said the same thing you just said. He's absolutely opposed to the idea. He tells me I need a more straightforward, normal sort of marriage, and I guess it's natural for a radical pragmatist like him to feel that way, but I don't really care if he approves or not. In the spring of next year, when my betrothed graduates, we're going to decide things for ourselves." She squared her shoulders, looking adorably determined. I forced a smile and just kept nodding as she spoke. What I envied most was her beautiful innocence, which made my own old-fashioned, hidebound mentality feel like an ugly thing. Following that afternoon of revelation, Serikawa-san and I were never again as close as we had been. Women are strange. Two girls can have the most intimate friendship, but bring one man into the mix and they can suddenly become very stiff and formal, treating each other as virtual strangers. For us, the change wasn't that extreme, but we began to be more reserved with each other, more polite in our greetings, less chatty, and generally more "mature." We both avoided discussing the subject of the photograph.

And so the months passed, and soon enough Serikawa-san and I both entered the spring of our twenty-third year. It was an evening in late March, to be more exact, when this strange thing happened. At about ten o'clock that night, Mother and I were in the living room, sewing Father's serge overkimono, when the maid softly opened the shoji screen and beckoned to me. *Me?* I asked with my eyes, and she gave me two or three quick little nods. Mother pushed her eyeglasses up to rest on her forehead and said, "What is it?" The maid gave a small cough. "Yes, Ma'am. Serikawa-sama, of the Kazuki-Do, is at the door." Looking quite uncomfortable, she coughed discreetly again and added, "He'd like to have a word with the young lady." I stood right up and went into the corridor, feeling as if I already knew what this was about: Serikawa-san had created some sort of problem. I headed toward the parlor, but the maid stopped me, telling me in a hushed voice that he was at the kitchen door. She trotted ahead in a tense crouch, as if on a vital mission. Serikawa-san's elder brother was standing in the dim light outside the kitchen door, smiling. Back when I was commuting to girls' school, he and I used to exchange greetings every morning and evening as I passed the Kazuki-Do, where he was always buzzing about with the shop boys, busily taking care of every detail. Even after I graduated, he would drop by the house once a week or so to deliver confectioneries we'd ordered, and I had always familiarly addressed him as *Nii-san*, or "big brother." But he had never dropped in so late at night before, and the fact that he had quietly asked to speak to me in particular convinced me that the Serikawa-san time bomb had finally exploded.

"I haven't seen your sister recently," I blurted out, before he said anything.

"Did you already know about all this?" he asked, eyeing me dubiously for a moment.

"No!"

"Oh. Well, she's gone. The idiot. Nothing good comes from this literature crap. You must have known something about what was going on?"

"Yes, well ..." My voice got tangled up in my throat. "I did."

"She ran off. I have a pretty good idea where she's gone to, but you haven't heard anything, right?"

"No. She's been rather distant lately. But what could have happened? Would you care to come in? I have so many questions."

"Thanks, but I can't be dawdling. I have to go find her

right away." He was dressed in a suit, I noticed now, and carrying a small suitcase.

"So, you have an idea where she is?"

"Yes. I'm going to give them both a good thrashing. Then I'll force them to marry."

After saying this, Nii-san laughed in a disarmingly carefree way and took his leave. I stood there in the kitchen doorway, vacantly gazing after him, then went back to the living room and sat quietly down, pretending not to notice my mother's questioning looks. I added two or three stitches to the sleeve I'd been working on, and then I stood quietly up again, walked to the corridor, and trotted mincingly back to the kitchen door. I stepped outside, slipping into my geta clogs, and set off running with complete abandon. What had got into me? To this day, I don't understand what I was thinking. In my mind, I was going to catch up to Nii-san, cling to him, and never let him go. The Serikawa-san issue meant nothing; all I wanted was to see Nii-san again. *I'll do anything, Nii-san, I'll follow you anywhere, take me away, just as I am, and ravish me!* I was burning that night in the sudden flames of a delusion that was mine alone. Silently I raced down the dark, winding paths, like a dog on the hunt, tripping and stumbling here and there, then straightening my kimono and running on, tears welling up and spilling down my face. I felt as if I were scouring the bowels of hell. When I reached the streetcar stop at Ichigaya-mitsuke, I couldn't catch my breath, my body ached, and the world went dark and murky before my eyes; I believe I was on the verge of fainting. Not a soul was at the streetcar stop. It looked as if the car had just left. In a final act of desperation, I took a deep breath and shouted at the top of my lungs: "NII-SAN!" Silence. I crossed my arms, turned, and headed home, smoothing my hair and clothing on the way, and when I got there I quietly opened the shoji to the main room. Mother peered suspiciously at my face and said, "What happened?" I told her without emotion that Serikawa-san had left home. "Imagine that," I said and began sewing again. That's all there is to the story. Serikawa-san, as I said, married that handsome fellow and now lives in Korea. I myself met and married my husband the following year. As for Serikawa-san's brother, from then on I felt nothing in particular when we met. As the new master of Kazuki-Do, he's more prosperous than ever and has found himself a petite and pretty wife. And all this time he's continued to personally deliver sweets we've ordered once a week or so. Nothing much has changed. Perhaps I nodded off that night while sewing and dreamed it all. The memory is awfully vivid to have been a dream, though. Does it make any sense to you? It's a story that seems like a lie, I know. But I ask you to keep it a secret in any case. My daughter is about to enter her third year of girls' school, you know.

## KATYDID

I'm leaving you. You've done nothing but lie to me. Maybe I'm partly to blame, but I don't really see what I've done wrong. Besides, I'm twenty-four now. Even if someone were to tell me what I'm doing wrong, I wouldn't be able to change. To change now, I'd have to die and be resurrected, like Christ. But to die at one's own hand seems to me the greatest of sins, so I've decided to leave you instead and to begin living the sort of life I feel is correct. I'm sure the rest of the world sees nothing wrong with the way you've chosen to live, but the truth is, you scare me, and I simply can't go on like this.

It's been five years since I came to you. We were formally introduced in the spring of my nineteenth year, and not long after that we married. When I moved in with you, I brought virtually nothing but the clothes on my back. I don't mind telling you now that both my father and mother were very much opposed to our marriage. Even my little brother, who'd just entered university at the time, seemed uncertain. "Are you sure you know what you're doing, Sis?" he'd say, sounding very grown-up and concerned.

I never told you this because I thought it might be unpleasant for you to hear, but I had two other prospective suitors at the time. I don't remember much about them, but I do remember being told that one of them had just graduated with a degree in law from the Imperial University. My big sister in Ikebukuro was the one who'd recommended him. He was from a good family and was studying to become a diplomat. I saw a photograph. He had this beaming, optimistic sort of face. The other man, who was nearly thirty, was an engineer in my father's company. Again, this was five years ago, so I don't remember all the details, but I seem to recall that he was the eldest son of a wealthy family and a man of very solid character. My father liked him, apparently, and he and Mother really pressured me to meet this one. I flatly refused, however, and I don't think I ever even saw a photograph. None of this really matters, of course. I'm only telling you what I remember about these men because it hurts when you just laugh and don't take me seriously. And I'm not saying all this to spite you. Please believe me. Not for a moment would I be so wanton and frivolous as to wish I'd married someone else. I can't imagine being with anyone else. You mustn't laugh as you always do. I'm saying these things in complete seriousness. Please hear me out to the end.

Back then I had no desire to be with anyone but you, and this much, at least, hasn't changed. Make no mistake about that. Ever since I was a child, the one thing I could not abide in people was indecisiveness. My father, my mother, and my sister in Ikebukuro were eager for me to find a husband and kept urging me to at least just *meet* this or that man. But to me a formal introduction seemed virtually the same as an engagement ceremony, so I was not about to "just meet" anyone. I had absolutely no intention of marrying either of those men. If they were as perfect as everyone said, then surely they could find any number of excellent candidates. They wouldn't need to have me in particular, and that's why they didn't interest me. I had this vague idea that I wanted to marry someone for whom – I know you're going to laugh when I say this – someone for whom, of all the women in the world, no one but me would do.

It was just as all this was going on that your name came up. It seemed an outrageous proposition, and Mother and Father were put off from the start. I mean, imagine: Mr. Tajima the antiques dealer comes to Father's office to show him a painting, and after rambling on and on the way he does, he says, "This painter is going to make a name for himself soon. Perhaps your daughter," et cetera. My father just wrote it off as some sort of ill-considered

jest, although he did buy the painting to hang on the wall
of his reception room. But what did Mr. Tajima do but
come back two or three days later and ask my father, very
formally and seriously, if he could arrange for the two of
us to meet. It was scandalous. Mother and Father were
shocked, not only at Mr. Tajima's brazenness – acting as
the go-between for a proposal like that – but at the man
who'd presumably put him up to it. Afterwards, of course,
when I asked you, I found out you'd known nothing about
it, that it was all Mr. Tajima's idea, something he'd done
simply because he was so devoted to you. Mr. Tajima has
helped us in so many ways. Without him, could you have
succeeded as you have? He even neglected his own business for your sake. That's because he believed in you,
right? You mustn't ever forget what he's done for you.

I was somewhat taken aback when I heard about his
crazy suggestion, but before I knew it I found myself wanting to meet you. For some reason the whole idea made
me happy, and one day I went to Father's office to steal
a look at your painting. Did I ever tell you about that? I
pretended I had some business with Father and stepped
into the reception room. It was really cold that day, and
I stood there alone, shivering in the corner of that big,
unheated room, as I drank the painting in. A little garden
next to a sunlit veranda. There's no one sitting on the
veranda, just a single white cushion. It's all in blues and

yellows and white. As I gazed at it, I began to shiver and tremble even more, so much that I feared I was going to faint. It seemed to me that I was the only one in the world who could truly understand that painting.

I'm saying all this in earnest. You mustn't laugh. For two or three days after that, day and night, I couldn't stop trembling. I *had* to become your bride, no matter what. That's how I felt. When I asked Mother to arrange a meeting, I burned with shame, knowing how wanton it would sound to her. She didn't answer but gave me a fierce scowl. I'd expected as much, however, and wasn't about to give up. I decided to meet with Mr. Tajima in person. He shouted "Bravo!" and jumped up but tripped over his chair and fell flat on his backside. It sounds comical now, but neither of us laughed at the time.

Of course, as you know, my family's opinion of you just grew worse with each passing day. Mother and Father kept coming to me with unpleasant facts they'd uncovered about you. God only knows how they went about investigating it all, but they found that you'd left your parents' home by the Inland Sea and had come to Tokyo without their consent, that you'd alienated not only your parents but all your relatives, that you were a drinker, that you'd never had a single one of your works in an exhibition, that you were apparently a leftist of some sort, that it was questionable whether you'd actually graduated from the art academy, and on and on. But thanks to Mr. Tajima, who patiently kept pressing the issue, we somehow finally managed to arrange a meeting. I remember it all vividly, upstairs at the Senbiki-ya restaurant. Mother went with me. You were exactly as I'd imagined you. I remember being impressed by how clean your shirt cuffs were. I could have died when I lifted my cup of tea and was trembling so much that the spoon clattered on the saucer. When we returned home, Mother made it clear that she now disapproved of you more than ever. What seemed to upset her most was that you'd just sat there smoking cigarettes and didn't even try to carry on a decent conversation with her. She kept saying that you had an evil face. And that you had no future. But I had made up my mind to marry you. I sulked for a month, and finally my parents gave in. We talked it over with Mr. Tajima, and then I came to you, as I said, with virtually nothing but the clothes on my back.

The two years we lived in the apartment in Yodobashi were the happiest years of my life. Every morning I woke up full of joy just thinking about the day ahead. You painted only what you wanted to paint, without concerning yourself in the least with who's having exhibitions, and who's moving up in the art world, and so on. The poorer we became, oddly enough, the happier I was. Even carrying things to the pawn shop and the used-book store gave me a warm kind of feeling. It was as if I'd finally found a home in this world. And whenever we ran entirely out of money, I looked upon it as an opportunity to test my own resources. It gave me a tremendous sense of purpose in life. After all, food is never as tasty, or as much fun to eat, as when you're just scraping by, right? I devised one delicious meal after another, didn't I?

But now I can't do anything. There's no need to use my imagination when I can just purchase whatever I want. I go to the market feeling perfectly empty and buy what all the other housewives are buying. I hate to say it, but ever since you suddenly became such a big deal and we moved to this house in Mitaka, there hasn't been any real joy in my life. I no longer have a chance to show what I can do, to test my own creativity. And you? You suddenly became such a smooth talker, and even though you acted even more thoughtful and caring towards me than before, it only made me feel like a pet cat or something. I'd never dreamed you were someone who'd get ahead in the world. I thought you'd live in poverty till the day you died, that you'd go on painting your willful, self-indulgent paintings and being the object of everyone's scorn but never letting that bother you and never bowing down to anyone. That you'd drink when you pleased and go through life without ever being muddied by the ways of the world. I believed – and I still believe – that there must be at least

one such noble person living on this earth. But no one
else, I told myself, would be able to see the laurel crown
on that man's head; he'd be treated as an outcast and a
fool, and I'd be the only one who would want to marry
him and take care of him. And that's exactly what I'd do,
I used to think: I'd spend my life serving him. I thought
you were that person, that angel. And I thought I was the
only one who could understand you.

But what happened? Suddenly you became this big, important man. And that, for me, is the root of the problem.

It's not that I begrudge you your success. In the beginning, as more and more people came to love those won-
drously sad paintings of yours, I gave thanks to God every
night. I felt so happy that at times it brought tears to my
eyes. During our two years in Yodobashi you painted whatever you felt like painting – the back garden you loved so
much, the streets of Shinjuku late at night – and when we
ran completely out of money, Mr. Tajima would show up
and leave a fairly large sum of cash in exchange for two or
three of your works. In those days you seemed indifferent to money, and you always looked so forlorn whenever
he left with your paintings. Mr. Tajima would call me out
into the hall, where he'd bow and thank me, very formally,
and then slip a white envelope into my sash. You always
acted completely unconcerned about how much he'd left,
and I was never so vulgar as to rip open the envelope and

count it in front of you. It was my intention to carry on whether we had money or not, and I never even told you how much he gave us. I didn't want to soil you with such things. And not once did I ever urge you to make more money or try to become famous. In fact, forgive me, but I was convinced that an inarticulate, coarse-mannered man like you couldn't possibly become wealthy and celebrated. But it was all just an act, wasn't it? Why? *Why?*

What a dandy you became after Mr. Tajima told you about his plan for the one-man show! First you started going to the dentist. Your teeth were so decayed that you looked like an old man whenever you smiled, but that had never bothered you before. When I used to suggest you see a dentist you only made jokes, saying that once all your teeth fell out, you'd get a whole set of ivories, or that there was no point in flashing gold caps and attracting all the ladies. But then, suddenly, you started visiting the dentist between paintings and coming back each time with one or two shiny new gold teeth. I'd say, "Let's have a look. Smile," and your cheeks would turn red beneath your beard and you'd make excuses in a timid tone of voice I'd never heard you use before, saying things like, "That damn Tajima keeps nagging me to get 'em fixed."

Your one-man show was in the autumn of our second year in Yodobashi, and I was thrilled about it. Why shouldn't I be happy if even one more person came to love your work? My eye for art had been validated, after all. But when the newspapers praised you so lavishly, and all the paintings in the exhibition sold, and you started to get letters from famous painters, it was all just a little *too* good, and it scared me. You and Mr. Tajima both kept urging me to go to the gallery for a look, but all I could do was sit in my room, knitting. Knitting and trembling from head to toe. Just to imagine it – a room with twenty or thirty of your paintings lining the walls, and a big crowd of people ogling them – was enough to make me want to burst into tears. It even seemed to me that so much good fortune, coming so soon, could only mean something terrible was bound to happen, and every night I asked God for forgiveness. "We have more than enough happiness now," I'd pray. "Please watch over him, and don't let anything bad happen."

You started going out every night with Mr. Tajima to be introduced to other famous artists. It never really bothered me, even when you didn't return until the following morning. But whenever that happened you'd make a point of telling me all about the previous night, saying So-and-So Sensei was this or that, or what a moron Mr. Something-or-Other was, and chattering on about the most trivial things, nothing like your normal, taciturn self. Until then, during the two years we'd been living together, I'd never heard you talk behind anyone's back that way. You, with your lofty independence, were supposed to be above caring what So-and-So Sensei was like, weren't you? Worse, though, was that by chattering away about the previous night, you seemed to be trying to convince me that you'd done nothing wrong. I wasn't born yesterday. If you just told me the truth instead of making feeble, roundabout excuses, it might be painful for me for a day or so, but in the long run it would be easier on my feelings. After all, I'm your wife. I never had much faith in men when it came to things of that nature, but then I've never been overly suspicious either. I don't worry about that sort of thing. It's something I could grin and bear, and at this point, it's the least of my worries.

Suddenly we were wealthy, and you were terribly busy. The Nika School welcomed you as a new comrade, and you began to feel embarrassed that we were living in such a small flat. Mr. Tajima kept urging you to move, saying that people would wonder how much confidence they could put in you if you remained in such a place, and the prices of your paintings would never take off. He said you should rent a large house as an investment. You became quite enthusiastic about this disgusting little scheme, saying, "Yeah, you're right – the bastards just look down on a guy who lives in a place like this." Crude remarks of this sort gave me chills and made me feel horribly alone. Mr. Tajima rode his bicycle all over town looking for a house for us, and finally discovered this place in Mitaka.

We had few belongings when we moved at the end of the year, but then, without even consulting with me, you went around buying all sorts of lavish furnishings. When they started delivering these things, one after the other, I felt so sad I could have sat down and cried. Before I knew it, I had become what I'd always despised: the "lady of the house." You even suggested we hire a maid, but that was where I drew the line. I'm not a person who is capable of ordering others around.

Shortly after we moved, you had three hundred New Year's cards printed, each one doubling as a notice of our new address. Three *hundred*. At what point had you acquired so many acquaintances? It seemed to me you were in terrible danger, like a man walking a tightrope, and I was so afraid for you. I was sure something disastrous would happen at any moment. You weren't the sort of man who could survive in a world of such superficial socializing. That's what I thought, and I spent each day ridden with anxiety over it. But not only did you avoid a fall, good things just kept happening to you. Is it me who's got everything backwards?

My mother started coming to visit every few days, bringing clothes I'd left behind, or my passbook, or this or that, and she was always in the best of spirits. As for Father, though at one point he'd grown to dislike the painting in the reception room so much that he'd put it in storage, he now had it set in a splendid new frame to hang prominently in his study. My sister, for her part, began writing letters, saying "keep up the wonderful work" and so on. We suddenly had lots of visitors crowding into the sitting room too, and I'd stand in the kitchen and hear you laughing merrily away. You really became quite the talker, didn't you? You used to be such a quiet person. I always thought it was because you understood so much about the world and saw how vain and silly everything is, but that's not the way it was at all, was it?

The things you say in front of your guests! Solemnly repeating, word for word, some theory of painting you heard from someone who'd visited just a few days before, as if it were your own well-considered opinion or, for example, when I mentioned my impression of a story I'd read, and the next day you calmly repeated my silly ideas in front of guests, saying, "After all, Maupassant too had a horror of religious belief, didn't he?" I was serving the visitors tea when I heard you say that, and I was so mortified I stopped dead in my tracks. You've simply never had any ideas of your own, have you? Forgive me. I hardly know anything either, but at least I'm capable of speaking for myself, whereas you're either completely silent or mouthing someone else's words. And yet you've achieved all this unaccountable success. Your painting in the Nika exhibition that year was awarded first prize, and the newspaper went so overboard in praising your work it was embarrassing: "noble solitude," "ascetic purity," "deeply contemplative," "melancholia," "prayerlike," "Chavannesque" – tossing around words like that. Later you were talking with a guest about that article and you said it "seemed fairly accurate." What a thing to say! We are not living a life anyone could call ascetic. Shall I show you our bank statement?

You seemed to change completely when we moved here. You began to talk about financial matters all the time, and now whenever a guest asks you to paint something for him, the first thing you do is name a price. You tell him that by deciding on a price beforehand, both of you can avoid any unpleasant misunderstandings afterwards. I must say I don't enjoy hearing you discuss such things. Why do you have to be so concerned with money? It's my belief that if you simply paint good pictures, the bread-and-butter part will take care of itself. What could be more satisfying than doing good work and remaining unknown, living in honest poverty? I want to live a quiet life, with a lofty but inconspicuous sort of inner pride. You've even gone so far as to check to see how much cash I have in my own pockets. When a sum of money comes in, you split it up and put some in that big wallet of yours and some in my little purse. You put, say, five large bills in your wallet and one large one, folded twice, in my purse, and the rest you deposit at the bank. And I just sit there, watching. Remember how upset you were that time I left the cash drawer on the bookshelf unlocked? I was flabbergasted by your reaction. When you go to collect money from a gallery now, you end up not coming home for two or three days. And as soon as you return – drunk, in the middle of the night, rattling the front door – you say the most pathetic things. "Hey, look, I've still got three hundred yen left over. Go on, count it." But it's your money, isn't it? Why shouldn't you spend as much as you like? I'm sure there are times when you want to squander money, as a sort of release. Are you afraid I'll begrudge you that? I understand the value of money. But I don't go through life thinking about nothing else. When I see you looking pleased with yourself because you've still got three hundred yen left, it just makes me feel unendurably alone.

I haven't the slightest desire for money. There's nothing I want to buy, nothing I want to eat, nothing I want to see. I can make do with old, worn-out furniture and cooking utensils, and I don't need any new kimonos because I can always mend or re-dye the ones I have. I've always known I'd get by somehow. I don't even like buying a new dish towel. It feels extravagant. You've taken me into the city to eat at expensive restaurants from time to time, but the meals in those places have never struck me as being the least bit delicious. I never feel comfortable; I just sit there with my heart in my mouth, and it all seems such a waste. Rather than bringing home three hundred yen, or taking me to a fancy restaurant, how much happier I'd be if you'd make a cucumber trellis in the garden. As strong as the afternoon sun is on the veranda, I'm sure cucumbers would do well out there. But when I begged you to build one, you just told me to hire a gardener. I wasn't about to hire some gardener, the way rich people do. I wanted *you* to make the trellis. But you just kept saying, "All right, all right, next year for sure," and now, after all this time, you still haven't done it. You squander so much money on yourself, but when someone else is in need, you act as if there's nothing you can do. When was it that your friend Mr. Amamiya came to ask your advice because his wife was ill and he was hard up for cash? You called me into the sitting room and asked me, with a perfectly serious face, if we had any money in the house. It was so bizarre, so absurd, that I didn't know what to do. I stood there turning red and fidgeting, and you said, "Don't hold back on us, now – if you dig around, you're bound to come up with twenty yen or so." I was appalled. Twenty measly yen. I looked at you, and you waved your arm as if to sweep away my gaze and said, "Never mind, just get it, don't be so stingy." And then you smiled sadly at Mr. Amamiya and said, "It's at times like this that we both feel the sting of poverty." I was dumbfounded. Ascetic purity? Ha! Melancholia – is there even a trace of anything so noble in you, the way you are now? You're just the opposite: a happy-go-lucky egotist. When you're bellowing that silly song in the washroom every morning – "Say you believe me, baby!" – I just feel so ashamed, wondering what the neighbors must think. Prayerlike, Chavannesque – words like that are wasted on someone like you. Noble solitude? Doesn't it ever occur to you that you're spending your life surrounded by sycophants? The visitors call you Sensei, and you sit there and disparage everyone else's paintings, one after the other, as if no one else were walking the same lofty path as you. But if you really feel that way, there's no need to criticize others so indiscriminately, much less intimidate others into agreeing with you. Where's the "noble solitude" in that? Why must you try to impress everyone who comes by?

You're a liar. That's what you are: a despicable liar.

It was such a miserable time for me last year when you broke away from the Nika School and started your own group, the "New Romantics" or whatever you call it. Forming the group with the very people you'd been making fun of for so long, behind their backs. You don't have any fixed opinions of your own, do you? None whatsoever.

Could it really be that your way of life is what the world considers correct? When Mr. Kasai comes to visit, the two of you heap scorn on Mr. Amamiya, but when Mr. Amamiya comes by you're terribly kind to him and tell him that when all is said and done, he's your only true friend. You say these things with such emotion that it all rings true, and then you start criticizing Mr. Kasai. Do all successful people act this way? How do they keep from slipping up? It's incredible to me, and horrifying, to think that anyone could carry on this way without eventually stumbling and falling. Something bad is going to happen. And you know what? I almost hope it does. For your sake, and as proof that God really does exist, I've reached the point where, in some dark corner of my heart, I pray that something awful will befall us. But nothing ever does. Only good things, one after another. The first exhibition of works by your group seems to have been praised to the skies. As for your *Chrysanthemums*, I heard some of our guests talking about how your spirit had reached new levels of purity, and how the work "exudes a fragrance of rarefied, exalted love." What's going on here? I just don't understand.

During New Year's you took me along for the first time when you paid your respects to the famous Okui-sensei, who's always been the most ardent supporter of your work. A renowned master like that, and he lives in a house that is, if anything, smaller than ours. That man is what I call the real thing. The way he plopped his portly body down, sitting cross-legged on his cushion, looking as if nothing could budge him, and peering at me through his spectacles with those big eyes of his – those were the eyes of a man who knows the meaning of noble solitude. I began to tremble all over, just as I had when I first saw that painting of yours in my father's freezing reception room. Okui-sensei spoke about simple, everyday topics, in a completely unaffected way. And what did you say when he looked me over and made a joke about what a fine catch you'd made, saying I looked like samurai stock? In a proud and perfectly serious voice, you said, "Yes, her mother descends from samurai." I broke out in a cold sweat at that moment. My father and mother were both commoners to the bone. I wouldn't be surprised if before long you started telling people my mother's from the aristocracy. It's frightening, and it's a mystery to me why a man like Okui-sensei can't see through your phoniness. Or is that just normal behavior for people in this world? Sensei kept sympathizing with you, saying how hard it must be to get your work done these days, but when I thought about that silly song you sing every morning, I couldn't help wondering what was what. It struck me as so preposterous, I nearly burst out laughing. And then, after we left Sensei's house, before we'd walked even a block, you kicked at the gravel in the road and said, "What a sentimental old git. Getting all weak-kneed over a woman." I was shocked by your cowardice: one minute you're groveling in front of that splendid old gentleman, and the next you're stabbing him in the back. You must be insane.

It was at that moment that I decided to leave you. I couldn't endure it any longer.

You even seem to have forgotten how much you're indebted to Mr. Tajima. "That idiot Tajima came by again the other day" – you say things like that to your so-called friends, and at some point it seems Mr. Tajima caught wind of it. Now when he visits, he comes through the rear entrance, laughing and announcing, "The idiot Tajima's back again!" I just don't understand you people at all. What in the world has happened to your pride? Sometimes I wonder if you and your friends aren't tormenting me intentionally. The other day you were on the radio, talking about "The Significance of the New Romantic Movement for Our Times," or something similarly self-congratulatory. I was in the living room, reading the newspaper, when out of the blue I heard your name being announced, and then heard your voice. It was almost like the voice of a complete stranger. So thick and garbled and nasty-sounding. *What a disgusting person*, was my instinctive reaction. I was able to see you clearly, to put you in perspective, at that moment: you're just an ordinary man. But I have no doubt that you'll continue to get ahead in the world. It's all so ridiculous. Over the radio I heard you say, "I am what I am today because..." And that's when I switched it off. Who in heaven's name do you think you are? Have you no shame? "I am what I am today" – don't ever utter such horrifyingly moronic words again! Ah . . . I hope you trip up, and soon.

That night, I went to bed early. When I turned off the lights and lay down on my back, I heard a cricket singing its heart out. I guess it had made its way under the veranda, and now it was directly beneath me. It felt to me as if an invisible katydid were singing from deep in the core of my spine. And I resolved to remember that faint little voice for the rest of my life, to keep it there, locked up inside, as I made my way in the world. It's a world where, I suppose, you are the correct one and I'm the one who's mistaken, but I just can't see it. I don't see where my mistake is, or what's wrong with my way of thinking.

# CHIYOJO

Let's face it, women are no good. Or is it just me? I can't speak for all women, but it's beyond doubt that I, for one, am no good. And yet, even as I say this, an obstinate sort of self-belief, deeply rooted in some dark, hidden corner of my heart, insists that at least there's one good thing about me ... And that only leaves me all the more confused about myself, trapped in this oppressive, intolerable state of mind. It's like having my head stuck in a rusty old cast-iron pot. I'm a stupid person. Genuinely stupid. And in the new year I'll be nineteen. I'm no longer a child.

When I was twelve, my uncle in Kashiwagi submitted a student composition of mine for a contest sponsored by the magazine *Blue Bird*. My piece was awarded first prize, and one of the judges, a famous author, went hideously overboard in praising it, and I've been a mess ever since. That composition of mine is just embarrassing to me now. Was it really all that special? What was supposed to be so good about it? Titled "Errand," it's a simple story about being sent to buy some Bat cigarettes for my father. When the tobacco-shop lady handed me five packets, it made me a little sad that all of them were the same pale green color, so I exchanged one for a different brand in a vermilion packet. But then, sadly, I no longer had enough money. The lady just smiled, however, and said I could make it up next time, which was awfully nice of her and made me really happy. When I balanced the four green packets on the palm of my hand and placed the vermilion one on top, it looked like a blossoming primrose, so pretty that my heart seemed to skip, and I could hardly walk straight. That's the gist of the piece, which I now find mortifyingly childish and cloying.

But it wasn't long after that, at the urging again of my uncle in Kashiwagi, that I submitted another composition of mine, titled "Kasuga-cho," and this time it was published not in the "Readers' Submissions" section of the magazine but on the very first page, in big, bold lettering. The story begins with my aunt in Ikebukuro moving to Kasuga-cho in Nerima. She told me about the big garden in her new house and invited me to visit her there, and so, on the first Sunday in June, I boarded a train at Komagome Station, transferred to a Tokyo-bound train at Ikebukuro, and got off at Nerima Station, where I saw nothing but fields all around me. I had no idea which direction Kasuga-cho might be, and when I asked people working in the fields, none of them seemed to know, and I ended up fighting back tears. It was a very hot day. The last person I asked was a man of about forty who was pulling a cart filled with empty cider bottles. He stopped, flashed a lonely smile, and used a gray, soiled hand towel to wipe the sweat dripping down his face. He thought for some time, muttering "Kasuga-cho, Kasuga-cho . . ." Finally he said, "Kasuga-cho long way from here. You catch east train there, Nerima Station, east train to Ikebukuro. Transfer train to Shinjuku. At Shinjuku transfer local train, get off Suidobashi . . ." and so on, doing his best to give me these detailed directions in very broken Japanese. I knew right away that he was thinking of the other Kasuga-cho, the one in Hongo, but I also realized he was Korean, which touched my heart and made me all the more grateful to him. The Japanese people I approached feigned ignorance because they couldn't be bothered, while this man from Korea, dripping with the sweat of his labor, takes the time to really try and help me. His information was wrong, of course, but I thanked him for his kindness and followed his directions, walking back to Nerima Station and jumping on a train for Tokyo. I seriously thought about going all the way to Kasuga-cho in Hongo, but that would have been silly, so I went straight home instead. Once there, I felt sad and out of sorts and decided to write down an honest account of what had happened. This account is what was published in huge print on the front page of the *Blue Bird*, and that's when all my troubles began.

Our house is in Nakazato-cho in Takinogawa. My father, who teaches English at a private university, is a son of Tokyo, but Mother was born in Ise. I have no older siblings, just a physically infirm little brother who entered middle school this year. By no means do I dislike my family, but I'm so lonely. Things were better before. They really were. Mother and Father both spoiled me rotten, and I was always joking and making everyone laugh. I was an excellent older sister too, very kind to my brother. But soon after my composition was featured in the *Blue Bird*, having won me another prize, I transformed into a truly cowardly, hateful creature. I even began talking back to my mother and arguing with her. The famous author Iwami-sensei, who was one of the judges, published in the same issue a commentary on "Kasuga-cho" that was two or three times the length of the story itself. It made me so sad when I read it. I felt as if I'd somehow deceived this great man, who was clearly a modest person with a heart much purer and more beautiful than mine.

And then, at school, Mr. Sawada brought the magazine to our composition lesson and copied out the entire text of "Kasuga-cho" on the blackboard, working himself into quite a lather as he harangued us for an hour, bellowing praise for each sentence. I could have died. I had difficulty breathing, the world went dim and hazy before my eyes, and I had this horrifying sensation that my entire body was turning to stone. I knew I didn't deserve all this praise; and what would happen the next time I wrote something mediocre or worse? Everyone would laugh at me, and it worried me half to death to think how embarrassing and painful that would be. Even at that tender age, I could tell that Mr. Sawada wasn't impressed with the composition itself so much as with its having been featured prominently in the *Blue Bird* and lauded by the celebrated Iwami-sensei. But this realization only made me feel all the more unbearably alone. And the thing is, everything I was worried about actually ended up happening, in one painful, embarrassing scene after another. My friends at school suddenly began distancing themselves from me, and Ando, who had been my best friend, mocked me relentlessly, calling me "Ichiyo-san" and "Murasaki Shikibu-sama" and so on. Finally she stopped associating with me altogether, taking up instead with the Nara and Imai crowd, whom she'd previously despised. They'd huddle together, stealing glances at me and whispering, making nasty remarks, and bursting into squeals of laughter.

I told myself I'd never write another composition as long as I lived. Urged on by my uncle in Kashiwagi, I had submitted the piece without really thinking, and it was a big mistake. This uncle of mine is my mother's younger brother and works at the ward office in Yodobashi. He's thirty-four or -five and fathered a baby last year, but he thinks he's still young and sometimes drinks too much and raises a ruckus. Whenever he comes to our house, he leaves with a handful of cash Mother slips him. When he entered university his plan had been to study to become a novelist, and although his teachers and mentors had high hopes for him, according to Mother, he fell in with an un-savory crowd and ended up dropping out of school. He ap-parently reads tons of novels, by both domestic and foreign writers, and he's the one who urged me to send my stupid composition to the *Blue Bird* seven years ago and who's made my life miserable in so many ways ever since. I didn't like literature. I feel differently now, but at the time, with my silly compositions having been featured in two consec-utive issues of the magazine, with my friends turning on me, and with my teacher openly giving me unwarranted special treatment, it was all just too much, and I came to hate even the thought of writing. I was determined that no matter how my uncle flattered and cajoled me, I would not be submitting any more works. When he pushed me too hard, I would just start wailing at the top of my voice and put an end to it. During composition class I didn't write a single word but would doodle circles and triangles and paper-doll faces and things. Mr. Sawada called me into the teachers' room one day and scolded me about my attitude, saying that there's a difference between self-respect and arrogance. It was absolutely humiliating.

I was about to graduate primary school, however, after which I hoped incidents like this would be behind me. And indeed, once I began commuting to the girls' school in Ochanomizu, I was relieved to find that not a single person in my class knew about my stupid essay having won some contest. In composition class I wrote with a carefree attitude and was happy to receive average marks. But my uncle in Kashiwagi continued to tease and badger me relentlessly. Every time he came to our house he would bring three or four novels and order me to dive in. I generally found these books difficult to understand and often just pretended to have read them when I handed them back.

When I was in the third year of girls' school, my father received, totally unexpectedly, a long letter from the famous Iwami-sensei, the judge who'd selected and lauded my submission to the *Blue Bird*. In the letter, he called me a "rare talent" and said a lot of things I'm too embarrassed to repeat, praising me ridiculously and saying it would be a pity to waste such a gift. He urged my father to have me write more pieces and offered to help get them published. It was a serious letter, written in formal, self-effacing language that we were hardly worthy of. Father handed it to me without saying anything. When I read it, I once again felt admiration for the excellent sensei, but reading between the lines it was clear to me that my uncle's meddling was behind this. He had somehow contrived a means to approach Iwami-sensei and trick him into writing the letter. I was certain of this, and I told my father as much. "Uncle put Iwami-sensei up to it. I have no doubt about that. But why would he do such a creepy thing?" I was near tears and looked up at Father, who gave me a little nod, showing me that he too had seen through it. And he didn't look happy. "Your uncle in Kashiwagi means well, I'm sure," he said, "but he's put me in a difficult position. How am I supposed to reply to such a great man?"

I don't think Father had ever liked this uncle of mine much. When my composition was selected, both he and Mother had been thrilled and celebrated noisily, but Father alone protested, yelling at my uncle, saying that all this excitement was not in my best interest. Mother told me about this afterwards, sounding very disgruntled. She often speaks ill of her little brother, but she blows up when Father criticizes him in any way. My mother is a good, kindhearted, cheerful person, but it's not uncommon for her and Father to get into arguments about this uncle of mine – the Satan of our family. Two or three days after we received Iwami-sensei's courteous letter, they got into a terrible shouting match.

We were eating dinner when Father broached the subject. "Iwami-sensei has kindly gone out of his way to write such a heartfelt letter," he said. "I'm thinking that, in order to avoid seeming disrespectful, I need to take Kazuko and pay him a visit, so we can apologize and she can explain exactly how she feels. Just writing a letter could give rise to misunderstandings, and I wouldn't want to offend him in any way."

Mother lowered her eyes and thought for a moment before saying, "My brother is to blame. Forgive us for all the inconvenience." Then she raised her head with a little smile, dragged a straggling lock of hair back in place with her pinkie finger, and went on, speaking rapidly. "I guess it's because we're just a pair of fools, but when Kazuko was so extravagantly praised by the famous Sensei, we naturally wanted to ask his continued blessings. We wanted to try to keep things rolling, if possible. You're always blaming us, but aren't you being a little obstinate yourself?"

Father paused his chopsticks in midair and spoke as if delivering a lecture. "Trying to 'keep things rolling' is pointless. There's a limit to how far a girl can go in the field of literature. She might be briefly celebrated for the novelty of it all, only to find afterwards that her entire life has been ruined. Kazuko herself fears this. The best life for a girl is to have a normal marriage and become a good mother. You two only want to use Kazuko to vicariously satisfy your own vanity and ambition."

Mother paid no attention to what he was saying but turned away to reach for the hot pot on the charcoal bra-

zier, then let go and cried out. "Ow! I burned myself."
She put her index finger and thumb to her lips. "But,
listen. You know my brother has no ill will in all this."
She was still not facing Father, who now set his bowl and
chopsticks down.

"How many times do I have to say this?" he shouted.
"You two are preying on her!"

He adjusted the frame of his glasses with his left hand
and was about to continue, when Mother suddenly let out
a keening wail that quickly deteriorated into sobs. Dab-
bing at her eyes with her apron, she began bringing up
financial matters, openly disparaging Father's salary and
our clothing budget and I don't know what. Father looked
at me and my brother and with a jerk of his chin ordered
us to leave. I took my brother to the study, where for a
full hour we heard them yelling at each other in the living
room. My mother is normally an easygoing, openhearted
person, but when she gets agitated she can say things so
reckless and hurtful that it makes me want to stop up my
ears with candle wax. The next day, on his way back from
teaching, Father called on Iwami-sensei at his home to
express gratitude and apologize. That morning he had
encouraged me to accompany him, but the thought
of it frightened me so much that my lower lip started
trembling and wouldn't stop, and I just didn't have it
in me. Father returned at about seven that evening and

reported that "Iwami-san," though surprisingly young, was a splendid gentleman who fully understood how we felt, to the extent that *he* ended up apologizing to Father, saying that he hadn't really wanted to encourage the girl to pursue literature but had been asked repeatedly to write that letter and had finally done so, albeit reluctantly. He didn't name the person who'd put him up to it, but obviously it was my uncle in Kashiwagi. Father explained all this to Mother and me. When I surreptitiously pinched the back of his hand, I saw him wrinkle his bespectacled eyes in a little smile. Mother listened, nodding calmly as he spoke, and had nothing to say in response.

For some time after that, my uncle didn't come around much, and when he did, he treated me rather coldly and didn't stay long. I forgot all about composition. When I got home from school each day I'd tend to the flower garden, run errands, help out in the kitchen, tutor my younger brother, sew, study my lessons, massage my mother's shoulders, and so on. I was busy each day trying to be of service to everyone, and that kept me motivated and enthusiastic.

Then came the storm. At New Year's when I was in my fourth and final year of girls' school, my primary school teacher Mr. Sawada paid us a visit. Mother and Father were taken aback somewhat but pleased to see him again and wined and dined him generously. Mr. Sawada told

us he'd quit teaching primary school and was now working as a private tutor and living a more carefree life. He
certainly didn't strike me as being carefree, however. I
had assumed that he was about the same age as my uncle, early forties at most, but now you might have taken
him for fifty-something. He had always looked older than
he was, I suppose, but in the four or five years since I'd
last seen him he seemed to have aged about twenty. He
came across as exhausted, lacking the strength even to
laugh; and whenever he tried to force a smile, his hollow cheeks were creased with deep wrinkles. I didn't feel
pity for him so much as a kind of repulsion. He still wore
his hair closely cropped, but it was predominantly white
now. He praised me personally, which he'd never done
when I was his student, and it left me somewhat confused
at first, and then very uncomfortable. He remarked on
how pretty I was, how ladylike, and so on – transparent
flattery, delivered with an absurd degree of deference,
as if I were somehow above him. He gave Mother and
Father a frightfully tedious account of my primary school
career, focusing on my compositions, which I, for one,
had already happily forgotten about.

"Such a waste of talent." he said. "At the time, I was not
particularly interested in juvenile compositions and knew
nothing of the teaching method by which creative writing
can actually be used to enhance a child's innocence and

wonder. I have a firm grasp on the subject now, however, having done extensive research, and I'm confident in my mastery of the latest methods. What do you say, Kazuko-san? Why not have another go at studying composition under my tutelage? I can guarantee..." blah, blah, blah. He was quite inebriated by now, having drunk several cups of sake. Sitting with one fist on his hip, elbow out, he concluded this grandiose nonsense by insisting we shake hands to seal the deal. Mother and Father were smiling, but I could tell they didn't know what to make of all this. Unfortunately, as it turned out, Mr. Sawada's proposal wasn't just drunken bluster. Ten days or so later he showed up at our house, acting as if we'd been expecting him.

"Very well. We'll start by going over the fundamentals of composition," he announced.

I was flabbergasted. I later found out that Mr. Sawada had found himself in trouble over something to do with entrance exams and had been forced to resign from the school, after which, in order to survive, he'd begun making the rounds of his former students' homes, presenting himself as a highly qualified tutor and pressuring the families to hire him. Shortly after visiting us at New Year's, it seems he discreetly wrote a letter to Mother, once again enthusiastically praising my so-called literary talent. He also informed her about the current popularity of the essay form and the recent ascendance of a number of young girls who were being acclaimed as literary geniuses. He was obviously trying to entice her into contributing to his scheme. Since Mother, for her part, still retained lingering regrets about my abortive literary career, she promptly fell into his trap, writing back to ask if he'd be willing to give me weekly lessons. She told father that her main intention in doing so was to offer some assistance to Mr. Sawada in his efforts to support himself, and Father reluctantly agreed, apparently feeling that it would be wrong to refuse a man who had once been my teacher. Such was the situation, and from then on Mr. Sawada showed up each Saturday to lecture me in the study, where he would proclaim the most ridiculous nonsense. I hated every minute of it.

"To master writing, the first thing one needs is a solid grasp of the use of postpositions." He'd make obvious statements like this and then beat them into the ground, as if they were matters of supreme importance. "'Taro plays in the garden,' right? *Taro wa niwa* wo *asobu,* is incorrect. *Taro wa niwa* e *asobu,* is also incorrect. *Taro wa niwa* nite *asobu'* is the proper way to say it." When I giggled at these ludicrous examples, he glared at me reproachfully, as if trying to burn a hole in my face. Then he heaved a deep sigh and said, "Your problem is that you lack sincerity. However great a person's talent, without sincerity he or she will never achieve success in any field.

Are you familiar with Terada Masako, the one they call 'the baby-girl genius'? Born into an impoverished home, the unfortunate child's greatest desire was to study, and yet she lacked the means to purchase so much as a single book. The one thing she did have, however, was sincerity. She faithfully followed her teacher's instructions, and that's why she was able to produce that masterpiece of hers. And her teacher too must have been a zealous fellow. If you had a little more sincerity in you, I'm certain I could make you every bit as successful as Terada Masako. In fact, because you happen to be blessed with favorable circumstances, I believe I can make you into an even greater writer than she is. Why? Because in one respect, at least, I'm more *advanced* than her teacher was. I'm talking about my grasp of moral education. Do you know who Rousseau was? Jean-Jacques Rousseau. He lived in the sixteen hundreds – or rather the seventeen ... Wait. Was it the eighteen hundreds? Oh, that's right, go ahead and laugh. Laugh your insincere little head off. You have some nerve, mocking your own mentor because you think all you need is your talent. Listen to me. Long ago, in China, there was a man named Gankai, who ..."

He would go on and on, talking about all sorts of random things, but as soon as an hour had passed, he'd switch it all off. "We'll pick up from there next week," he'd airily announce, then stroll out of the study into the living room, where he'd chat awhile with my mother before taking his leave. I know it's naughty to say things like this about a teacher from primary school, to whom I'm supposed to be indebted, but I couldn't help thinking that the man was losing his grip. He would flip through his little notebook, then come out with insanely obvious statements. "Description is an important part of writing," he said one day. "If the description doesn't work, readers won't know what you're trying to say." After returning the notebook to his breast pocket, he turned to look sternly out the window, where countless small snowflakes were drifting down, like something out of a Kabuki play. "For example, if you wanted to describe the way the snow is falling right now," he said, "it would be wrong to say it's falling *heavily*. That doesn't *feel* like snow. Falling *rapidly*? Same problem. How about *fluttering* down? Still not quite right ... *Sifting* down – now, that's close. Now we're zeroing in on the *feeling* of this snow. Yes, yes, very interesting." He waggled his head and crossed his arms, terribly impressed with himself. "*Softly* falling – how's that? Well, 'softly' is an adverb we normally associate with spring rain, so, no. Shall we settle on 'sifting,' then? Wait. 'Sifting softly' – combining the two might be one way to go. Sifting softly, softly sifting ..." He narrowed his eyes while whispering the words, as if savoring the taste of them. And then, suddenly, "No! Still not good enough. Ah! Do you know this line from the old Noh play? 'Like goose down, the snow scatters and swirls.' That's the classics for you – solid stuff. 'Goose down,' in and of itself, is a truly ingenious device. Kazuko-san, are you beginning to understand?" He turned to face me for the first time since peering out the window. I hated him and felt sorry for him at the same time and was nearly in tears.

In spite of scenes like this, I stuck it out for some three months, absorbing the same sort of dreary, unfocused drivel every Saturday, but eventually I couldn't bear even to look at the man's face anymore and told Father everything, asking him to put an end to Mr. Sawada's visits. Father heard me out and said that he hadn't expected this. He'd been against bringing in a tutor from the beginning but had gone ahead and agreed after being persuaded that it was primarily to help my former teacher support himself. He had no idea that I'd been receiving such irresponsible instruction; apparently he'd simply imagined that a weekly lesson from the man couldn't hurt and might even help me with my schoolwork. Once again, he and Mother got into a terrible quarrel over this. They were in the living room, but sitting in the study I could hear every word, and I ended up crying my eyes out. Knowing that all this turmoil was because of me, I felt like the worst, most unfilial daughter in the world. I even wondered if I should go ahead and wholeheartedly study the art of writing, if only to please Mother. But I knew I didn't have it in me. I couldn't write anything at all now, and in fact I never had possessed the literary talent some people ascribed to me. Even Mr. Sawada was better at describing falling snow than I, and I, who can't actually do anything, was the real fool for laughing at him. "Sifting softly" was a word picture I could never have come up with. Overhearing Mother and Father's shouting match, I couldn't help seeing myself as a truly horrible daughter.

Mother lost the argument that night, and we saw no more of Mr. Sawada, but bad things continued to happen. From Fukagawa in Tokyo emerged a girl of eighteen named Kanazawa Fumiko, who wrote beautiful prose that won universal praise. Her books sold far more than even those of the most celebrated novelists, and the rumor was that she became fabulously wealthy overnight. This was according to my uncle in Kashiwagi, who reported it to us triumphantly, as if *he* were the one who'd hit the jackpot. Listening to him, Mother got all worked up again. She babbled on enthusiastically as we cleaned up in the kitchen after lunch.

"Kazuko too has the talent to write, if only she'd try! What is your problem, Kazuko? It's no longer like the old days, when a woman had to confine herself to the home. You should give it another shot, and let your uncle from Kashiwagi guide you. Unlike Mr. Sawada, your uncle actually spent time in college, and you see all the books he reads. Say what you like, that makes him a lot more reliable. And if there's that much money to be made, I'm sure even your father will agree."

So my uncle once again began showing up at our house almost daily. He would drag me into the study to harangue me, saying things like, "First of all, you need to keep a diary. Just write what you see and feel. That alone can make for real literature." He also lectured me about a lot of difficult, convoluted literary theories, but I had zero interest in writing anything and let it all go in one ear and out the other. Mother is a person who'll get all excited about something but soon lose steam. Her enthusiasm this time lasted about a month before turning to indifference; but my uncle, far from cooling off, was now all the more determined to make me into a real writer, and announced as much with a perfectly straight face.

"Kazuko really has no choice but to become an author!" he shouted at Mother one day when Father was out. "Girls with this weird sort of intelligence aren't cut out for a normal marriage. Her only option is to give up on all that and devote herself to the artist's path."

Mother, understandably enough, looked offended at such an outrageous statement. "Oh?" she said with a sad smile. "Poor Kazuko. It doesn't seem fair."

Maybe my uncle was right, though. The following year I graduated from girls' school, and now, though I passionately despise his devilish prophecy, or curse, some small part of me wonders if won't prove to be true. I'm no good. I'm definitely stupid, and I'm not even sure who I am anymore. I changed, suddenly, after I finished school. I'm bored every day. Helping out in the home, tending to the flower garden, practicing the koto, looking after my brother – it all seems silly and meaningless. I'm now a voracious reader of scandalous, off-color books that I hide from my parents. Why do novels focus so much on exposing people's evil secrets? I've become an indecent girl who daydreams about unmentionable things. I now want to do just as my uncle taught me and restrict my writing to things I see and feel, as a way of asking God for forgiveness, but I don't have the courage. Or, rather, I don't have the talent. I can't bear this feeling, as if my head is stuck in a rusty old iron pot. I cannot write, even though these days I often think I want to try. The other day I broke in a new writing brush by scribbling in my notebook a piece I called "The Sleeping Box," about a trifling incident that happened one night. I later had my uncle read it, but before he got halfway through it he cast the notebook aside.

"Kazuko, it's past time for you to give up on the dream of becoming a lady writer," doing a stunning about-face and looking seriously fed up. It wasn't advice so much as an admonition. "Creating literature requires a special kind of genius," he informed me, with a wry smile. My father, on the other hand, takes a more lighthearted approach to it all, laughing and telling me that if I enjoy writing, I should go ahead and write. Mother sometimes hears gossip about Kanazawa Fumiko, or other young women writers who've become suddenly famous, and gets all worked up again.

"Kazuko, you could write just as well as this girl if you tried, but you don't have the tenacity to stick to it. Do you know the old story about Kaga no Chiyojo? Long ago, when Chiyojo first called on a great haiku master she hoped to study under, he gave her the task of writing a haiku with the title 'Nightingale.' She quickly turned out several attempts, but the master declined to approve any of them. So, what did Chiyojo do? She spent an entire sleepless night racking her brains, endlessly repeating the proposed title in her head, until she noticed that the sun was rising, at which point, without giving it any thought at all, she composed the famous 'Nightingale, I cry, / Nightingale, sing for me, and / now day is breaking.' When she showed this to the master, he praised her for the first time, slapping his knee and shouting, 'Chiyojo's done it!' Do you see what I'm trying to say? Perseverance is vital in all things." Mother takes a sip of tea after this pronouncement, then mutters the poem again under her breath. "'Nightingale, I cry, Nightingale, sing for me, and now day is breaking.' Brilliantly executed," she says, thoroughly impressed with her own story.

Mother, I'm not Chiyojo. I'm a dimwitted little imitation literary girl. Lying with my legs under the *kotatsu* covers to keep warm, reading a magazine and growing sleepy, it occurred to me that the kotatsu is a sleeping box for human beings, but when I wrote a story about that and showed it to my uncle, he tossed it aside without even finishing it. I reread the story later and realized he was right: it wasn't the least bit interesting. How does one become skilled at writing stories? Yesterday I secretly sent a letter to Iwami-sensei. "Please don't forget about the little girl genius of seven years ago," I wrote. I think I might be losing my mind.

# SHAME

Kikuko, I've shamed myself. I've shamed myself terribly.
To say it feels like my face is on fire is not enough. To say I
want to roll in a meadow screaming my lungs out doesn't
do this feeling justice. Listen to this verse from 2 Samuel
in the Bible: "And Tamar put ashes on her head, and rent
her garment of divers colours that was on her, and laid
her hand on her head, and went on crying." Poor Tamar.
When a young woman is shamed beyond all redemption,
dumping ashes on her head and crying her eyes out is a
proper response. I know just how she felt.

Kikuko. It's exactly as you said: novelists are human
trash. No, they're worse than that; they're demons. Horrible people. Oh, the shame I brought on myself! Kikuko.
I kept it secret from you, but I've been writing letters to
Toda-san. Yes, yes, the novelist. And then, eventually, I
met him, only to bring this horrible shame upon myself.
It's so insane.

164

Let me tell you the whole story, from the beginning. In early September, I mailed this letter to Toda-san. You can see how full of myself I was when I wrote it.

*Greetings. I'm aware that my writing to you may seem imprudent. You've probably never had so much as a single female reader of your stories and novels before. Most women only read books that are heavily advertised. They have no tastes of their own. Their choices are based on a kind of mindless vanity — "Everyone's reading this, so I too must read it." They have the greatest respect for pseudointellectuals, and they get all excited about pointless, tedious theories. You, on the other hand, if you'll excuse my saying so, wouldn't know a theory if you accidentally stepped in one. You're obviously no scholar. I began reading your novels in the summer of last year, and now I've read just about everything you've written. I don't need to have met you, therefore, to have a fairly complete picture as to your living conditions, as well as your physical features and general character. The fact that you have no female readers is, I believe, a defining characteristic. In your work you openly confess your poverty and stinginess; your selfish and vulgar marital spats; your unclean diseases; the ugliness of your features; the ragged filthiness of your clothes; the way you guzzle* shochu *while chewing on boiled octopus tentacles, only to end up in a violent rage; how you sometimes pass out and sleep on the bare ground; and how deep in debt you are. You disclose these and many other disgraceful and disgusting personal matters, all with unvarnished honesty. But let us be clear: on a personal level, none of this is appealing. Women, by nature, prefer cleanliness and purity. While I sympathize with you when I read how you're balding on top, and how your teeth are falling out, and so on, the overall picture is so distasteful that I can't suppress a wry smile, and — forgive me — I begin to feel contempt for you. And now you appear to be seeking female companionship in an establishment of a sort I decline to name. That's crossing a line, as far as I'm concerned, and at times I have to hold my nose as I read. It's only natural that any woman, without exception, would look down on and disapprove of you. I don't even let my friends know that I read your work. If they knew, I'm sure they would mock me, begin to doubt my character, and probably stop associating with me altogether. My hope is that you, for your part, will engage in a little self-reflection. While I acknowledge your innumerable faults — your lack of education, your clumsy writing style, your crude personality, your deficient ideology, your innate ignorance, and so on — I discovered, underneath it all, a strand of deep melancholia. Other women don't see this. Women, as I mentioned above, are motivated by vanity in their reading choices. They prefer idealistic novels, and stories about romance in elite summer resorts and such. But I believe that the melancholia underlying your work is something much more precious. Please do not lose hope on account of your unattractiveness, your past scandals, or your clumsy literary style; but treasure and preserve that uniquely melancholy spirit while taking better care of your health, learning a bit more about philosophy and language, and deepening your understanding of ideology. If your brand of pathos were to be wedded to a philosophical framework, I believe that your future work will no longer be the object of scorn, as it is today, and your own personal character might even be redeemed. When that day of redemption arrives, I will remove my mask, reveal my full name and address, and meet with you, but for now I shall merely cheer you on from the shadows. Allow me to be clear, however: this is not a 'fan letter.' Please do not go showing it to your wife or making crude jokes with your friends about having attracted a female fan. I too have my pride.*

*Kikuko.* That's more or less verbatim from my letter. I kept addressing him as *Kika*, which might be overly formal and a little awkward, but calling someone who's so much older *Anata* just felt too familiar. I didn't want him forgetting his age and getting any funny ideas, after all. That said, I don't respect him enough to call him Sensei;

and, besides, it would feel unnatural to use that form of address for someone with so little education. In any case, I had no misgivings after dropping this letter in the mailbox. I thought I had done a good deed. It lifts you up to lend even a small amount of courage to someone you can't help feeling sorry for. I didn't write my name or address on the letter, however. Well, I was afraid to! How shocking would it be for my mother if this man were to show up at our house, all drunk and disorderly. He might issue threats and demand we lend him money or something. After all, there's no telling what a man of such nasty habits might do, so I wanted to remain anonymous. But, Kikuko, that's not what happened. What did happen was horrible. And it left me with no choice but to write another letter. And this time, I stated my name and address clearly.

Kikuko, I'm such a pitiful child. When you hear what was in the second letter, you'll have a good grasp of the situation. Here goes. Please don't laugh.

*Toda-san. I'm flabbergasted. How did you manage to discover my true identity? Yes, my name is Kazuko. I'm twenty-three, and my father is a college professor. You did a brilliant job of unmasking me. I was dumbfounded to read your new story in* Literary World. *It made me realize that when it comes to novelists, one must never let down*

*one's guard. How did you discover all this about me?*
*You even saw into my feelings. "I've become an indecent*
*girl who daydreams about unmentionable things" — that*
*passage alone is a piercing arrow that serves for me as*
*proof of the astonishing progress you're made, and I'm*
*delighted to know that my anonymous letter inspired this*
*brilliant outburst of creativity. I never would have thought*
*that one woman's support could rouse an author to such*
*remarkable improvement. I have heard it said that with-*
*out the protection and comfort certain women offered*
*them, even such literary icons as and Hugo and Balzac*
*would never have been able to produce all those master-*
*pieces. Therefore, inadequate though my assistance may*
*be, I have made up my mind to help you. Please remain*
*strong. I will send you a letter from time to time. As for*
*your recent story, while the willingness to explore, to some*
*degree, the psychology of women is a step forward, and*
*while some passages were impressively adroit in this re-*
*spect, you still haven't quite "got it." I can teach you much*
*about what goes on in the heart of a young woman, being*
*one myself. I believe you to be a writer with tremendous*
*potential, and I have no doubt that your work will con-*
*tinue to improve. Please read more books and cultivate*
*your ability to employ logical reasoning. No one who*
*lacks sophistication can become a great author. Should*
*you face any painful difficulties, please feel free to write to*

*me. Now that you've seen through my mask, I will wear it no longer. My name and address are as indicated below. I'm not hiding behind a pseudonym. Don't worry. I look forward to meeting you one day, when you have reformed your character and fully redeemed yourself, but until then let us be content with correspondence. I must admit that what shocked me to the core was the fact that you knew even my name. I imagine that my letter stirred in you such a state of excitement that you showed it to your friends, perhaps asking an acquaintance at a newspaper to help you investigate the postmark and so on to track me down. Is that about right? It's despicable of men to make such a fuss over receiving letters from a woman. Please write back and explain how you knew my name and age. Let us correspond at length and, from here on, with kinder, gentler sentiments. And please take good care of yourself.*

Kikuko, I nearly cry, and feel as if I'm breaking out in a cold sweat, every time I reread this letter. Imagine this: I was completely mistaken. He wasn't writing about me. It wasn't about me at all. Oh, the shame. Kikuko, please feel sorry for me. I'm going to tell you everything.

Did you read Toda-san's story "The Seven Flowers of Spring" in this month's *Literary World*? A girl of twenty-three, who is afraid of love and thinks ecstasy detestable, ends up marrying a rich old man of sixty but soon becomes sick of this life and commits suicide. That's the story. It's a stark tale, very dark, with that distinctive Toda atmosphere. When I read it, I was convinced that the main character was modeled after *me*. I had read a mere two or three lines before it hit me, and I felt the blood drain from my face. After all, the character's name is the same as mine, and she's the same age. And her father is a college professor, just like mine. Aside from that, her life story is completely different from mine, but for some reason I was able to convince myself that things I had written had served as hints for even these embellishments. It's that naive credulity of mine that's the true source of my shame.

Four or five days later I received a postcard from Toda-san, and here's what he wrote:

*Dear Madam, I'm in receipt of your recent letter. Thank you for your support. I read your previous letter as well. I am not so lacking in common courtesy as ever to have shared a letter with my wife in order to ridicule anyone. Nor have I ever done so with friends. Please rest assured on that score. In reference to your offer to meet with me once my character is perfected, I can only respond by saying that I wonder if it's possible for any human being to perfect himself. Very sincerely yours, etc.*

That's a novelist for you, I thought: the man definitely has a way with words. It was a little annoying, but I had to admit he'd won that round. I thought it over for a day, and the next morning I woke up knowing that I had to go meet him. It was *essential* that I meet him. He was obviously suffering. If I didn't go to meet him right away, he might just fall completely apart. He was waiting for me to come. I would not let him down. I began getting ready immediately.

Kikuko, should a girl wear her finest clothes when calling on an impoverished author who lives in the tenements? Of course not. Remember the scandal that erupted when the head of a women's organization toured the slums sporting a fox-fur stole? One has to be mindful in these matters. According to his own writing, Toda-san hasn't even a proper kimono to wear, just an old padded robe that's leaking its cotton stuffing. The tatami mats in his house are worn to shreds, so the entire floor is covered with sheets of newspaper. I thought it would be unconscionable to show up at such an indigent household wearing, for example, the pretty pink dress I recently finished making, because to do so would only bring shame and sadness to the family. I put on an old, oft-patched skirt from my school days, and a yellow jacket I had worn skiing many years ago. This jacket was much too small now, and with its tattered sleeves reaching only halfway down my forearms, it fit the bill perfectly. I also knew from reading his stories that Toda-san suffers each year from the effects of beriberi, so I removed a blanket from my bed, folded it up, and wrapped it in a silk furoshiki to take to him. I planned to advise him to wrap his legs in the blanket when working. Not wanting Mother to notice and quiz me on where I was going, I slipped outside through the rear door. Kikuko, I think you know that one of my front teeth is removable; well, on the train I surreptitiously took it out, to make myself as ugly as possible. Toda-san, I knew, was missing many teeth; and so, in order to put him at ease and not shame him, I wanted to show him that my teeth were also a mess. I mussed up my hair as well, transforming myself into a homely, destitute woman. One needs to consider every detail when attempting to bring comfort to a weak, benighted, poverty-stricken individual.

Toda-san's house is outside the city. After transferring trains a couple of times I got off at the correct station, stopped at a police box to ask directions, and found the house easily enough. Kikuko. He doesn't live in a tenement building. He has a small but tidy little house of his own. The garden was beautifully manicured, with lots of autumn roses in full bloom. This was all totally unexpected. I slid the front door open to announce myself and saw chrysanthemums arranged artistically in a shallow bowl atop the shoe rack. A serene and very refined lady, who turned out to be Toda-san's wife, came to the entrance and greeted me, bowing politely. I wondered if I was at the wrong house.

"Excuse me, but would this happen to be the residence of the author Toda-san?"

"It is, yes."

"Is Sensei here?" I said, surprising myself by calling him that.

I was shown into the study, where I found a serious-looking gentleman sitting bolt upright at his desk. He wasn't wearing a padded robe. He wore a smart, dark blue kimono of a thick material I couldn't identify and a stiff black sash with a single white stripe. The study had the feeling of a tea ceremony room. In the alcove hung a scroll with a Chinese poem written in flowing calligraphy, of which I couldn't decipher a single character. A bamboo basket held a beautiful arrangement of ivy. Tall stacks of books stood next to the desk.

This was all wrong. He wasn't missing any teeth. He wasn't balding. He was clean cut and decent looking. Nothing about him hinted at uncleanliness. It was hard to imagine this person guzzling *shochu* and passing out in the dirt.

"This is different to what I expected from reading your stories," I said, after collecting myself.

"Is that so?" He didn't seem to have much interest in my expectations.

"How did you find out about me? That's what I came here to ask you." I was hoping to regain my bearings with this question.

No visible reaction. "I beg your pardon?" he said.

"I was concealing my name and address, but you found

out anyway. How did you do it? That was my first question in the letter I sent you the other day."

"Strange. I don't know anything about you." He looked directly at me with clear, untroubled eyes.

"My!" This was confusing. "If that's true, my letter couldn't have made any sense to you. Well! You might have at least told me that. You must have thought me a great fool."

I wanted to cry. How could I have been so deluded? What a horrible mess. Kikuko. To say I feel like my face is on fire is not enough. To say I want to roll in a meadow screaming my lungs out doesn't do this feeling justice.

"In that case," I said, "please return that letter to me. It's embarrassing. Give it back, please."

Toda-san nodded, with a grave look on his face. Maybe I had angered him. He must have thought I was an awful person.

"I'll look for it. I can't preserve all the letters I get each day, so it may be gone already, but I'll have my wife take a look. If we find it, I'll send it back. Or was it two letters?"

"Two letters, yes." I felt absolutely wretched.

"You say that something I wrote resembles your life story, but you need to understand that I never use real people as models for my characters. They're all made up, it's all fiction. And that first letter of yours ..." He stopped himself and bent his head.

"I apologize," I said. I was a poor beggar girl with

missing teeth. The sleeves of my too-small jacket were tattered. My navy-blue skirt was covered with patches. I could feel his contempt, from the top of my head to the tips of my toes. Novelists are demons! They're liars! He pretends he's poor when he isn't. He has fine features but tries to garner sympathy by saying his face is hideous. He's actually quite the scholar but feigns ignorance, claiming to have no education. He loves his wife but tells tales of fighting with her on a daily basis. He portrays himself as suffering deeply, and none of it is real. I'd been deceived. I stood up silently and bowed.

"Are you getting better?" I asked, before leaving. "With the beriberi and all?"

"I'm in excellent health."

I had brought this man a blanket. Now I was returning home with it. Kikuko, I was so ashamed of myself that, out on the street, I buried my face in that bundled blanket and cried my eyes out. A cab driver yelled at me: "Idiot! Look where you're going!"

Two or three days later I received by registered mail a large envelope. I guess I still had a glimmer of hope. Maybe Toda-sensei had written me some choice words that would relieve my shame. Maybe inside this oversize envelope I would find, in addition to my two letters, a thoughtful and comforting note from him. I pressed the envelope to my breast and said a little prayer, then opened it. It held nothing but my two letters. I carefully inspected the front and back of every sheet of my stationery, but he hadn't scribbled so much as a single word. The shame. You understand, don't you? I want to dump ashes on my head. I feel as if I've aged ten years. Authors are no good. They're human garbage. They write nothing but lies, and there's nothing romantic about people like this. Living comfortably in a normal household and callously looking down on a girl dressed in rags and missing a front tooth, not even seeing her off but acting utterly indifferent to her existence – how horrible can you get? Isn't this what they call fraud?

# DECEMBER 8

I'm going to take extra care in writing today's entry. I want to describe how one impoverished housewife of Nippon spent December 8, 1941. Then, if this diary of mine should be unearthed in the corner of some old storehouse a hundred years from now – when Nippon is celebrating 2700 glorious years since the founding of the Empire – it may be of some service as a historical reference, showing people what sort of life a housewife of our nation was living on this critical day. Poorly written though it may be, therefore, I must at least take care to write nothing but the truth. I don't want it to get all stiff and formal, however. According to my husband, there's nothing to be said for my letters and diary entries except that they're deadly serious; he says they lack feeling. It's true that from the time I was a little girl, I was concerned only with being well mannered, and though I'm not really all that serious deep down inside, I somehow become awkward when I try to express myself and can't seem to loosen up or let down my guard – something for which I'm forever suffering the consequences. Maybe it has to do with being too self-centered. I must make an honest effort to reexamine myself, especially now.

Speaking of the year 2700 reminds me of something rather silly that happened the other day. My husband's friend Mr. Ima came to visit for the first time in quite a while, and I had to laugh when I overheard him and my husband talking in the next room.

Mr. Ima said, "You know, this business about the next centennial founding day celebration has got me worried. It's really bothering me. Are they going to call it the year two thousand seven hundred or the year twenty-seven hundred? It weighs on my mind a lot. Doesn't it bother you?"

"Hmm . . ." My husband gave it some serious thought. "It does, yeah, now that you mention it."

"See what I mean?" Mr. Ima, too, was perfectly serious. "It seems they're going to call it twenty-seven hundred. That's the impression I get, somehow. But if I could have my way, I'd like it to be two thousand seven hundred. Twenty-seven hundred just won't do. It sounds indecent, don't you think? I mean, it's not a telephone number or something. I'd like them to say it properly: two thousand seven hundred. I wonder if there isn't something we can do to get people to say it that way when the time comes." He seemed genuinely concerned.

"However," my husband said, setting forth his opinion in a horribly pompous tone of voice, "they may have a completely different way of saying it a hundred years from now. Not two thousand seven hundred or twenty-seven hundred, but, for example *nunty* hundred . . ."

That's when I burst out laughing. How absurd can you get? My husband's always engaging in intense discussions with his visitors about things like this, things that don't matter one way or the other. A person with feeling is different from the rest of us, don't you know. My husband writes stories for a living. But it isn't much of a living, because he's forever loafing, and we just barely get by from day to day. I make a point of not reading his stories, so I have no idea what sorts of things he writes, but apparently they're nothing special.

Whoops. I'm digressing. At this rate, I'll never be able to write something good enough to last till the year 2700. I'd better start over.

December 8. Early this morning, as I lay in bed thinking about all the things I had to do today and nursing Sonoko (our baby daughter, who was born in June of this year), I clearly heard the words coming from one of the neighbors' radios: *The Imperial Headquarters of the Army and Navy have announced that as of shortly before dawn this morning, December 8, the Imperial Army and Navy have entered a state of war with British and American forces in the western Pacific.*

The words seeped through the slats in the rain shutters and into the darkness of my room with all the strength and clarity of sunlight. The announcement was repeated in the same crisp, crystalline tones. As I lay there quietly listening, my entire life changed. I felt as if I were being bathed in a powerful beam of light that left my entire body transparent. Or as if the Holy Spirit had breathed through me, leaving a single, cold flower petal lodged in my heart. Nippon too has changed. From this morning on, it's not the same Nippon.

I called to my husband, who was in the next room, to tell him the news, but no sooner had I spoken than he said, "I know. I know." His voice sounded grim and tense. Well, that's understandable. It was strange, though, that he, who always sleeps in, should have awakened so early. They say artists have strong powers of intuition, so maybe he had a hunch this was going to happen. I was rather impressed. But then he said something so foolish that it completely erased any admiration I might have felt.

"What d'you suppose they mean by 'the western Pacific'?" he asked. "The seas around San Francisco, maybe?"

What a letdown. I don't know how it happened, but

my husband hasn't the slightest knowledge of geography. Sometimes I'm not even sure he understands what "east" and "west" signify. I really began to wonder about him the other day, when he confessed that the way he'd learned it, the South Pole was the hottest place on earth and the North Pole the coldest. Last year he traveled to Sado Island, and afterwards he told me that when he first saw its outline from the steamship, he thought it was Manchuria. So you see how completely befuddled he is. How did he ever get admitted to university?

"The western Pacific is the side Nippon is on, right?" I said.

"It is?" He sounded disgruntled. "Well, that's news to me," he said, after mulling it over. "So America's in the east and Nippon's in the west? What a revolting idea. Nippon's supposed to be the land of the rising sun. The farthest east of the Far East. I always thought that Nippon is where the sun rises, and now you're telling me America's to the east of us? What an unpleasant thought. Isn't there some way of looking at it so we can put Nippon east of America?"

He says the strangest things. I'm afraid he's gone a bit overboard in his patriotism too. The other day, as he was nibbling on some salted bonito entrails, he launched into a truly bizarre boast: "The hairy barbarians, for all their swaggering, would never be able to swallow this stuff. But me? I could scarf down any Western food they set before me."

I didn't concern myself with his oddball grumblings this morning but got up and quickly opened the rain shutters. It was a fine day. But piercingly cold. The diapers I'd left out hanging under the eaves were frozen stiff, and the garden was covered with frost. The sasanqua were blooming, cold and white. It was so quiet. And to think that, at that very moment, war was raging in the Pacific. To the marrow of my bones I felt gratitude for this land, Nippon. I went out to the well and washed my face, and as I began rinsing Sonoko's diapers, the lady from next door came out. After we'd exchanged greetings, I said, "Well, it's not going to be easy from now on, is it?"

I meant the war, of course, but my neighbor had just recently been elected chief of the Neighborhood Association, and apparently she thought I was referring to that.

"Oh, well," she said, looking embarrassed. "It's not as if I can accomplish much anyway."

It was a bit awkward for me. Surely it's not that she isn't concerned about the war; it's just that she's anxious about the heavy responsibility she's taken on. I felt sorry for her. It really is going to be a difficult job now. If there should be an air raid or something of that sort, the responsibility of the chief is a truly serious matter.

At some point I may need to take Sonoko and evacuate

to the countryside, which would mean my husband would have to stay behind and protect the house. But he's so incompetent in so many ways, I hate to think about what could happen. He might not be of any use at all. I mean, he still doesn't even have a civilian uniform. What's he going to do if a worst-case scenario unfolds? He's so careless about these things. If I were to go out and get him a uniform, I'm sure he'd grumble about it – "What the hell's this?" – but he'd probably be inwardly relieved and go ahead and wear the thing. The problem is, he's so long and gangly I can't just buy one off the rack. It's a difficult situation.

He too got up at about seven this morning and, after a quick breakfast, got right to work. It seems he has a lot of little jobs he needs to finish up this month.

At breakfast I said, "Do you think Nippon will be all right?" It just slipped out.

"If not, we would not have acted," he said, sounding very formal. "Victory is certain." My husband is forever telling lies, and you can't trust anything he says. I decided that these particular words of his were ones I would take to heart, however.

While I was cleaning up in the kitchen afterwards, I thought about all sorts of things. Is it just the fact that the color of their eyes and hair is different that makes me feel such hostility toward the enemy? I want to see them beaten to a pulp. It's a completely different feeling from when we went to war with China. Just the thought of those callous, animallike American soldiers dragging their feet over the noble soil of Nippon is unbearable to me. Take one step on this sacred ground, you beasts, and your feet will rot out from under you. You're not worthy. To the lovely soldiers of Nippon I say this: Wipe the enemy out! From here on in, we at home may have to endure shortages of various kinds, but you needn't worry about us. We don't mind. We won't feel the least bit indisposed. None of us regret having been born in such difficult times. On the contrary, it's almost as if the times have given purpose to our lives. I, for one, am glad to have been born in this generation. Ah, I'd like to talk with someone about the war to my heart's content. *We did it, didn't we? It's finally started.* Like that.

From morning on, the radio broadcast one war song after another, giving it their all. One right after another, until finally – I don't know if they'd begun to run out of songs to play or what – they started broadcasting those ancient ones like "Though the enemy be tens of thousands." I had to laugh to myself. It was really quite endearing. My husband doesn't like radios, so we've never had one in the house. And I can't say I've ever wanted one all that badly myself. I do wish we had a radio now, though. I want to hear lots and lots of news. I'll talk it over with him. I have a feeling he'll let me get one now.

Along toward noon came a flurry of important announcements. I couldn't sit still, so I picked up Sonoko and went out to stand under the neighbors' maple tree and listen to their radio. Surprise invasion of the Malay Peninsula ... the attack on Hong Kong ... the Imperial Proclamation of War ... As I stood there listening with Sonoko in my arms, the tears started coming, and I didn't know what to do. I went back in the house, where my husband was still working, and told him all the news I'd just heard. All he did was smile and say, "Is that so?" Then he stood up, and sat back down again. He seemed kind of distraught.

Shortly after noon, having apparently finished one of the pieces he was working on, he gathered up the manuscript and dashed out. I suppose he was taking it to the magazine publisher's office, but judging from the way he flew off, as if making a getaway, I knew he wouldn't be home until late. He always returns late after fleeing the house like that. Not that I mind, of course, as long as he doesn't stay out all night.

After saying goodbye, I roasted dried sardines for a simple lunch, and then I strapped Sonoko to my back and went off toward the station to do some shopping. I stopped at the Kamei family's house on the way. We'd received a big box of apples from my husband's hometown in the country, so I'd wrapped a few to give to Yuno-chan (their pretty little five-year-old daughter). Yuno-chan was standing at the front gate when we arrived. As soon as she saw us, she ran to the door and called her mother, saying, "Sonoko-chan's here!" Apparently Sonoko gave Mr. and Mrs. Kamei a big smile from over my shoulder, because Mrs. Kamei made quite a fuss over her, saying how darling she was. Mr. Kamei, looking quite manly and valiant in work clothes and a jumper, explained that he'd been laying straw mats under the veranda.

"I tell you," he said, "crawling around under the veranda is a task comparable to landing on enemy shores. You'll have to excuse this filthy getup."

I wonder why he was spreading out straw mats under the veranda. Do they intend to crawl down there if we have an air raid? It's strange.

But I envy Mrs. Kamei. Her husband, unlike mine, really loves his family. I understand that he used to dote on them even more than he does now, but that after we moved into the neighborhood my husband began initiating him into the mysteries of alcohol and what have you, and he's not quite the man he was. I'm sure Mrs. Kamei bears a grudge against my husband, and I don't blame her.

All sorts of tools were lined up beside their gate: a flame beater, an odd-looking sort of rake, and so on. There's nothing like that at our house. But what can you expect with a husband as lazy as mine?

"My, you're certainly well prepared," I said.

Mr. Kamei smiled and said, "Well, after all, I am the chief of our Neighborhood Association."

Mrs. Kamei corrected him, saying in a gentle voice that he's actually the assistant chief, but the real chief is such an elderly person that Mr. Kamei has to do most of the work. Well, there's no denying that Mr. Kamei is a hardworking person. He and my husband are as different as night and day.

I excused myself, saying I had to be going, and they gave me some sweets to take home.

I went to the post office to pick up a payment of sixty-five yen from the magazine *New Tides*, and after that I went to the marketplace. As usual, there wasn't much to buy. I had no choice but to get cuttlefish and dried sardines again. Forty sen for two cuttlefish and twenty sen for a bundle of sardines. I heard more radio announcements outside the market.

Big news flashes, one after the other. Aerial attacks on the Philippines and Guam. The bombing of Hawaii. Total destruction of the American fleet. Official proclamations by the Imperial Government. I felt so grateful to everyone, I couldn't stop trembling. It was embarrassing. As I stood there listening, two or three ladies stopped beside me, saying, "Lets hear the news before we go." Those two or three became four or five, and soon I was standing in a crowd of ten or more people.

I left the marketplace and headed for the kiosk at the station to buy my husband's cigarettes. There was nothing different at all about downtown Mitaka. A big sheet of paper with the radio news written on it was posted in front of the greengrocer's, but the storefronts and the conversations of people were more or less the same as always. I found this calm atmosphere reassuring. Since I had a little more money than usual, I went ahead and bought myself a pair of sandals. I had no idea that, starting this month, there was a 20 percent tax on anything over three yen. I should have bought them at the end of last month. But then again, I think hoarding is despicable. The sandals cost me six yen, sixty sen. Before heading home, I also bought some cream for thirty-five sen and some envelopes for twenty-one sen.

Shortly after I got back, young Mr. Sato from Waseda University came by to say that now that he'd graduated, he'd decided to enlist in the army. It's too bad my husband wasn't home. I bowed deeply to the young man and said a prayer for his safety. And no sooner had he left than Mr. Tsutsumi from the Imperial University showed up. He too had graduated, but though he'd taken his physical for the draft, he'd been deferred. Both of these young men had always worn their hair rather long, but now their heads were shaved clean. It made a deep impression on me. Not even students have an easy road ahead of them now. It really was a shame my husband wasn't home, because late in the afternoon, Mr. Kon came by for the first time in a long while, twirling his walking stick. Having gone to the trouble to make the trip all the way here, to the outskirts of Mitaka, he had no choice but to turn around and go back without seeing his old friend. It made me sad just imagining how he must have felt on his way home.

As I was beginning to prepare dinner, the lady from next door came over to say that the sake ration coupons for December had arrived, but there were only six coupons to be divided among the nine households in the Neighborhood Association, and what should we do? I thought perhaps we should ration the sake on a first-come, first-served basis, but it seems all the families wanted some. We finally decided to split the six bottles into nine equal portions, which meant gathering some extra empty bottles and going straight off to Isegen to buy the sake. Since I was in the middle of preparing dinner, I was excused from helping. But once I had the meal under control, I put Sonoko on my back and went to see how things were going. The neighbors were arriving one by one, each carrying a bottle or two, and I was handed one also. Then, on the porch of the association chief's house, we started dividing the sake. We lined up nine bottles and carefully measured the volume by eye until they were all even. It isn't easy dividing six bottles of sake into nine.

Later, the evening paper came. It was four pages long, instead of the usual two, and how big the headline was!

EMPIRE DECLARES WAR ON U.S. AND GREAT BRITAIN

It was more or less the same news I'd heard on the radio, but I still read every word and got worked up all over again.

I ate dinner alone, then put Sonoko on my back and headed for the baths. Getting in the bath with Sonoko is the greatest pleasure of my life. She loves it, and when I put her in the water, she gets very quiet and still. She curls her hands and feet and peers up at my face. I suppose she wonders what's happening to her. Other women also seem to find their own babies irresistibly adorable – you see them pressing them to their cheeks and kissing them and so on. Sonoko's belly is as perfectly round as if it were drawn with a compass, and it's as white and soft as a new rubber ball. It's almost hard to believe that there's really a little stomach and intestines and everything inside there. And then, just below the center, is her tiny belly button, like a budding peach blossom. Her feet, her hands, everything about her is so lovely, so darling, that I just can't help but go into raptures. There isn't a kimono in the world you could put on her that would match the beauty of her birthday suit. When we get out of the bath and I dress her, I always feel a sense of regret. I always wish I could hold her naked body just a little while longer.

It was still light out when we went to the baths, but by the time we started for home, it was completely dark. Blackout. And now it's not just a drill. I felt a strange tightening in my chest. I took one step at a time, sort of feeling my way, but it's a long walk and before long I was getting a bit panicky. Coming out of the field and into the cedar grove was really something. It was absolutely pitch dark. It reminded me of how frightened I was when I was a student and crossed from Nozawa Hot Springs to Kijima on skis in a snowstorm. Instead of a rucksack, though, I had Sonoko on my back – sleeping, unaware of anything. Suddenly, from somewhere behind me, I heard a man singing, completely out of tune, "Summoned by-y-y His Ma-a-jes-ty," and walking with rough, shambling steps. Then he coughed in a certain way, and I knew who it was.

"This isn't easy for Sonoko," I said, and he answered in a booming voice.

"What the hell. You people don't have any faith – that's why you find it hard to walk along a dark road like this. Me, I've got faith. For a man with faith, walking in the dark is the same as walking in broad daylight. Follow me," he said, and plodded on.

My husband. There's no telling to what extent he's actually in his right mind.

# WAITING

Every day I come to this little National Railways station to meet someone. Someone – I don't even know who.

On my way home from shopping I always stop here to sit on this cold bench, with my shopping basket balanced on my lap, idly watching the ticket gate. Each time a train pulls into the platform, throngs of people burst out of its doors and come tramping toward the gate, all with angry looks on their faces as they flash their passes or hand over their tickets, glancing neither left nor right when they rush past my bench, making straight for the plaza out front, where they proceed to scatter in every direction. I just sit here vacantly. A person – one someone – smiles and speaks to me. Oh, how terrifying! Ah! What to do? My poor heart! Just imagining this scenario is like being doused with ice water; it's enough to take my breath away and send a shiver down my spine. And yet, here I am, still waiting for someone. Who in the world is this person I sit

193

here waiting for every day? What sort of person is it? Or is it even a person at all? I don't like people. Or, rather, I'm afraid of them. When I bump into an acquaintance and have to exchange pleasantries, halfheartedly saying things I don't even want to say ("How have you been? It's getting cold, isn't it?"), it makes me feel awful, as if I'm the biggest liar in the world, and I just want to curl up and die. Being subjected to mealymouthed flattery, or virtuous but insincere sentiments, and disheartened by the small-minded, overly cautious attitudes I encounter, I start to hate the world more than ever. Do we really have to wear ourselves out being so guarded with one another and exchanging such stiff, unnatural greetings, for our entire lives? I never enjoyed meeting up with people and never visited friends if I could help it. The thing I liked to do most was to stay at home with Mother, just the two of us, and sew. But when the big war started and the atmosphere around us grew so terribly tense, I began to feel anxious, to feel that there was something terribly evil about just sitting home dreaming my days away, and soon I found I couldn't relax. It occurred to me that what I really wanted to do was to work like a slave, in order to be of some use. I lost confidence in the life I'd been leading till then.

I couldn't just sit quietly at home anymore, and yet I had nowhere to go. So I'd go shopping for food, then stop at the station on my way back and plop down on this cold bench.

*Oh, if only someone would suddenly appear!* There's that sort of anticipation, coupled with this fear: *Oh no! What if someone really* does *appear?* Anticipation and fear and a kind of resignation, a feeling that there's nothing I'll be able to do but yield up my life to this encounter, that my fate will be sealed at that moment. Such thoughts occur to me, along with all kinds of absurd fantasies, all entwined together, filling my breast until I feel as if I'm going to suffocate. I'm not sure if I'm living or dead, or if I'm in the middle of a dream. It's a frightfully fragile and unreliable frame of mind. The people passing by begin to appear small and far away, as if I'm looking through the wrong end of a telescope, while a hush falls over the world. Oh, what is it I'm waiting for? For all I know, I might be a horribly indecent woman. Maybe all that stuff about suffering anxiety after the war started and wanting to work like a slave, to be of service, was a lie; maybe I saw this as an opportunity to construct a noble-sounding pretext for realizing my own wanton fantasies. It may be that even as I sit here with this vacant look on my face, the flames of some outrageous intrigue are flickering in my breast.

Who in the world am I waiting for? I have no clear image of who or what it is. It's all very hazy. I continue, however, to wait. Each and every day since the big war started, on my way home from shopping, I stop at this station, sit on this cold bench, and wait. Someone – one person – smiles and speaks to me. Oh, how frightening! Ah! What to do? No, no, you are *not* the one I'm waiting for! But who, then, *is* the one? A husband. No. A lover. Nope. A friend. No thanks. Money. Hardly. A ghost. Oh no!

No, it's something more gentle, peaceful, brilliant, and wonderful, but I don't know what. Something like spring, for example. No, wait. New green leaves. The month of May. A crystalline stream in a field of barley. None of those are quite right either. Ah, but I'm still waiting. Waiting with a spark of hope in my heart. Right in front of me, crowds of people stream by. That's not the one; neither is this. Clutching my shopping basket and trembling, I wait and watch with every fiber of my being. Please don't forget me. Please don't laugh at me, but remember this poor twenty-year-old girl who visits the station each day to meet someone, only to return home alone, with nothing. I won't reveal the name of this little station. I don't need to; one day you'll see me here.

# ONE SNOWY NIGHT

It had been snowing since morning that day, you know. I'd finally finished the *monpe* trousers I'd been making for Otsuru (my niece), so on the way back from school I delivered them to my aunt's house in Nakano, and Auntie gave me two dried cuttlefish to take home with me. When I got to Kichijoji Station it was already dark and still snowing, softly, with more than a foot of snow on the ground. I was wearing boots, though, so I was glad there was so much snow and deliberately walked where it was piled up deepest. I'd been carrying the cuttlefish under my arm, wrapped in newspaper, and it wasn't until I got to the postal box near my house that I realized my package was gone. I'm a scatterbrained, silly girl, but I don't often drop or lose things. That night, however, maybe because I was so excited about frolicking in the snow, that's just what I did. I felt awful. I know it's rather unseemly to worry about a couple of dried cuttlefish, and I was ashamed of

197

myself for that, but I'd been planning to give them to Kimiko, my big brother's wife. She's going to have a baby this coming summer. They say that when you have a baby inside you, you tend to get very hungry, because now you need to eat enough for two people. Kimiko isn't like me at all, she's very refined and elegant and careful about her appearance, and until now she always ate "like a canary," as they say, and never snacked between meals or anything, but lately she says she gets so hungry it's embarrassing, and she suddenly gets cravings for the strangest things. That's where the cuttlefish comes in. Just the other day, as Kimiko and I were cleaning up after supper, she was sighing and muttering to herself that she had this bitter taste in her mouth and wished she had some dried cuttlefish or something to chew on. And then, just by coincidence, Auntie in Nakano gave me those two cuttlefish, and naturally I couldn't wait to hand them to Kimiko. So you see why I felt so bad when I realized I'd dropped them.

As you know, in our household it's only my big brother, Kimiko, and I, and my brother is kind of strange. He's a novelist, well into his thirties but not the least bit famous, and he never has any money. He spends most of his time in bed, and though he claims that it's because of failing health, his mouth is healthy enough, and he's always bawling us out about one thing or another, although, for all his complaining, he never does anything to help us out around the house, so that Kimiko has to do even the heavy work, the man's work, and you can't help but feel sorry for her. One day I got so indignant about it all that I said to him, "Why don't you go out to the country with a rucksack and bring back some vegetables or something once in a while? I believe other men do that."

He got very cross and huffy.

"Fool! I'm not grubby and common like some people, that's why. Listen – and you remember this too, Kimiko. Even if we were starving to death in this house, you wouldn't catch me pulling some low-minded stunt like that, joining those food-hunting mobs, so resign yourselves to that right now. There are some things I'll never stoop to."

That might come across as admirably self-sacrificing, I suppose, but in my brother's case you can't tell if it's motivated by patriotism or just plain laziness. My father and mother were both from Tokyo, but Father worked for the government up north in Yamagata for many years, and my brother and I were both born there. My father died in Yamagata, and when my brother was about twenty and I was just a baby, Mother brought us back to Tokyo. Mother too passed away a few years ago, and now it's just my brother and Kimiko and I, and since we don't have any roots in the countryside, we never get food sent to us from relatives the way other families do; and my brother, being such an oddball, doesn't have any actual friends, so nobody ever calls on us unexpectedly to say they've managed to get their hands on some rare treat, and that's why I couldn't help thinking how happy Kimiko would be if I presented her with something, even a couple of dried cuttlefish – and it may be grubby and common of me, but I felt so bad about dropping them that I turned right around and retraced my steps.

It was hopeless, though. To find something wrapped in white newspaper on that snow-covered street would have been difficult even if it weren't still snowing and piling up like that, and I walked all the way back to Kichijoji Station without seeing a trace of my package. I sighed, tilted my umbrella back and looked up at the dark night sky. The snowflakes were dancing crazily around in the air, looking like a million fireflies. It was so pretty. The trees on either side of the street were covered with snow, their branches hanging down heavily and stirring softly from time to time, as if sighing. It was like being in some sort of fairyland, and I forgot all about the cuttlefish. And then, suddenly, I had a wonderful idea: why not take this beautiful snowy night back home to give to Kimiko? That would be so much better than any old cuttlefish! To focus only on food *was* low-minded, if you thought about it. Shameful, really.

My brother once explained to me that your eyes can

store the things you look at. He said the proof was that if you look directly at a light bulb, even briefly, then close your eyes, you can still see the bulb on the inside of your eyelids. Then he told me this little story about something he said once happened in Denmark. My brother's stories usually just come off the top of his head, and you can't believe a word of them, but I thought the one he told me that time, whether he made it all up himself or not, was worth remembering.

Long ago, according to the story, a doctor in Denmark did an autopsy on a sailor who'd been shipwrecked, and when he studied one of the sailor's eyeballs under a microscope, he found a lovely little family scene imprinted on the retina. The doctor reported this strange finding to a writer friend of his, and the writer soon came up with an explanation. The shipwrecked sailor, he said, had been swept up by giant, raging billows and smashed against a rocky seaside cliff. Dazed and frantic, he clung tightly to what he thought was a rock, only to find that it was the window ledge of a lighthouse. Rejoicing, the sailor was about to call for help when he happened to glance through the window and saw the lighthouse keeper and his family sitting down to a modest but cozy dinner. Ah, thought the sailor, if I scream for help now, I'll disrupt the wonderful harmony this family is enjoying. And just then his fingers began to slip from the ledge, and another great wave came along and washed him out to sea. The writer said that this was undoubtedly what had happened, and that the sailor had been the gentlest, most noble-hearted man in the world. The doctor agreed, and the two of them saw to it that the sailor received a proper burial, along with a reverent eulogy.

That's the story, and it's one I like to believe. Even if it's scientifically impossible, I still want to believe it. And so, having suddenly remembered the story, I decided to imprint that beautiful snowy night on my retinas. Then, when I got home, I'd have Kimiko look in my eyes, to make sure she has a beautiful baby.

See, a few days ago, Kimiko told my brother to hang pictures of beautiful faces on the wall of her room. "I want to look at them every day," she said, smiling, "so my baby will be pretty too."

My brother nodded very seriously and said, "Hmm. Pre-natal conditioning, eh? You're right, that is important."

Later he put pictures of two Noh masks on the wall – Magojiro and Yuki no Ko-omote. Both are classical beauties, of course, but then he ruined everything by hanging a photo of his own scowling face right between them. Meek and mild though she is, not even Kimiko could put up with that.

"Please," she said, practically begging him, "not that picture of you. It makes me feel all queasy inside."

She did finally get him to let her take it down, thank goodness. I mean, if she had to look at a photo of my brother every day, her baby might come out looking like a little monkey or something. Is it possible that my brother, who has one of the strangest faces you'll ever see, thinks of himself as being on the handsome side? What can you do with someone like that? At any rate, all Kimiko wants to do, for the sake of her baby, is to gaze at the most beautiful things in the world. That's why I wanted to imprint this snowy night on my eyes and take it back to show her. I was sure it would make her much happier than any dried cuttlefish ever could have.

So I gave up on the search and headed home, and on the way I opened my eyes wide to let in all the lovely, pure white scenery around me, and by the time I reached our house I felt as if the snowy images were imprinted not only in my eyes, but way down deep in my heart.

"Kimiko!" I called out as soon as I got home. "Come look in my eyes. My eyes are full of the most beautiful scenery!"

"What? What *ever* are you talking about?" Kimiko stood up, smiling, and put her hands on my shoulders. "Something happened to your eyes?"

"Don't you remember that story he told us? About how the things you've been looking at remain inside your eyes?"

"Your big brother? I'd forgotten about that. After all, most of his stories are nonsense, you know."

"Yes, but that one story is the truth. At least, I want to believe it is. So look into my eyes. Please? I've just seen the most beautiful snowy night. Look close. That way you'll have a baby as perfect as a snowflake."

Kimiko was staring at me with a sort of sad, thoughtful smile on her face when my brother barged in from the next room. "Hey," he said, "there's no use looking into those boring eyes of Shunko's" (that's my name). "Looking into my eyes will be a hundred times more effective."

"Says who?" I shouted. My brother was so hateful to me right then, I could have hit him. "Kimiko says it makes her feel queasy to look in your eyes."

"Ha! Not likely. My eyes have seen twenty years' worth of beautiful snows. I lived in Yamagata till I was twenty, Shunko. You don't even know what that incredible Yamagata snow is like. We moved to Tokyo when you were still too little to know anything. Getting all worked up about some piddling Tokyo snowfall. Pshaw! My eyes have seen a hundred, no, a thousand times more snowy scenes than yours have, more than I even care to remember – and prettier ones too. Say what you will, your eyes aren't even in the same league as mine."

I was so enraged by this that I wondered if I should just go ahead and burst into tears. But then Kimiko saved me. She smiled gently and spoke in a quiet voice.

"Maybe your eyes *have* seen a thousand times more pretty things than Shunko's, Papa, but they've seen a thousand times more ugly, disgusting things too."

"That's right! Kimiko's right! And the ugly things outnumber the pretty things by far! That's why your eyes are all yellow and cloudy! So there!"

"Cheeky little brat," he growled, and skulked back into the other room.

# LA FEMME DE VILLON

I.

I'm awakened in the middle of the night by the sound of the front door clattering open. I know it's only my husband coming home drunk, however, and just lie here quietly in bed.

He switches on the light in the next room, and I can hear him panting noisily as he rummages through the drawers of his desk and bookcase, searching for something. Then he plops down heavily on the tatami mats, and all I hear is his husky, rapid breathing. I wonder what he's up to.

"Welcome back. Did you eat dinner? We have rice balls in the cupboard."

"Oh. Thank you," he says, in a gentle tone I'm not accustomed to hearing from him. "How's the boy? Still got a fever?"

This too is unusual. Our son will be four next year, but

whether because of a lack of nutrition, or his father's al-
coholism, or some sort of disease, he's smaller than most
two-year-olds and still can't walk very well. As for talking,
the best he can manage is "Yum-yum!" and "No!" and
the like. I fear something's wrong with his brain. When
I take him to the public bath and hold his naked body,
he's so heartbreakingly tiny and withered that I've been
known to burst into tears, right there in front of everyone.
He's sick a lot too, forever getting an upset stomach or
breaking out in a fever.

My husband rarely spends any time at home to speak
of, and I have no idea what he thinks about all this. I'll
tell him the boy is running a temperature, and he'll say
something like, "Oh? Maybe you should take him to the
doctor," then throw on his inverness and head off for
parts unknown. I'd love to take the boy to a doctor, but it's
not as if we have the money or means to do so. The best
I can do is lie down beside him and stroke his little head.

But tonight, for some reason, my husband asks about
the boy's fever and sounds genuinely concerned. That
ought to make me happy, but instead I have this ominous
feeling, and a chill runs up my spine. I'm lying here listening to my husband huff and puff, not knowing what
to say, when I'm startled by the reedy voice of a woman
at the front door.

"Excuse me."

A shiver runs through me, as though I've been doused with cold water.

"Excuse me! Ohtani-san?"

There's a little more edge to her voice now. I hear her slide the door open, and this time, in a decidedly angry tone:

"Ohtani-san! We know you're in there!"

At this point, my husband finally goes to the door.

"What? What is it?" he says, very awkward and apprehensive.

"As if you don't know," the woman says, lowering her voice. "Why would a man with a fine house like this be stealing things? Stop with the nasty pranks and give it back. Give it back, or we're going straight to the police!"

"What are you talking about? How dare you. You people have no business coming here. Go away, or *I'll* be the one bringing charges."

Now another male voice speaks up.

"Sensei, you're got some nerve. We have no business coming here, you say? How are we even supposed to reply to that? Taking money from someone else's house is no joke! Don't you realize how much trouble you've caused us already? And now you pull a disgraceful stunt like this. I really misjudged you, Sensei."

"It's extortion," my husband proclaims, but his voice is quivering. "Blackmail is what it is. Get out of here. If you've got a problem, we can talk it over tomorrow."

"Just listen to you, Sensei. You're a full-fledged criminal now. I guess we have no choice but to go to the police."

The hatred in the man's voice gives me goosebumps all over.

"Go to hell!" my husband says, in a hollow screech.

I get up, throw a wrap over my nightgown, and go to the entrance.

"Good evening," I say to the two visitors, and bow.

"You must be the missus," the man says, acknowledging me with a grim nod. He's at least fifty, with a round face, and he's wearing a knee-length overcoat.

The woman is forty or so, small, thin, and neatly dressed.

"Forgive us," she says, "for disturbing you at this time of night."

She doesn't smile but uncovers her head, letting her shawl fall to her shoulders, and returns my bow.

That's when my husband suddenly steps into his geta clogs and tries to dash out the door.

"Oh no you don't!"

The man grabs him by the arm, and the two of them grapple for a moment.

"Let go of me! Let go, or I'll stab you!"

A jackknife glitters in my husband's hand. This knife is a prized possession he usually keeps in his desk drawer. I recall him rummaging through the drawers when he got home and realize that he must have been expecting a confrontation like this and stuffed the knife in his pocket.

The man steps back, and my husband takes that opportunity to fly out the door, the cape of his inverness flapping like the wings of a giant crow.

"Thief!" the man shouts. He's about to give chase, but I jump down to the dirt-floor entryway in my bare feet and throw my arms around him.

"Let him go. We don't want anyone getting hurt. I'll take care of this."

"She's right," says the woman, off to the side. "It's a madman with a knife. There's no telling what he'll do."

"Damn it! I'm going to the cops, though. Enough is enough!"

Gazing out at the darkness, the man mutters these words as if to himself, but I can feel the tension drain out of him.

"I'm so sorry," I say to both of them. "Please come in and tell me what this is all about." I step up into the room, then sit on my knees facing them. "Perhaps I can help. Do come in. The place is a mess, but ..."

They look at each other and exchange a nod. The man gathers himself and clears his throat.

"In any case," he says, "our minds are made up. You may as well know the whole story, though."

"Yes. But do come in, so we can discuss this at our leisure."

"This is no time for leisure," the man says, but begins to remove his overcoat.

"You might want to leave your coat on. It's so cold, and we haven't any heat in the house. Please, just as you are."

"Very well then, if you really don't mind."

"Not at all. You too, ma'am. Please."

The man steps up into the room – the six-mat room my husband uses – and the woman follows. They both seem to gasp as they survey the squalor: the rotting tatami mats, the punctured paper screens, the flaking walls, the closet door with its framework exposed, the desk and the bookcase – the empty bookcase – in one corner.

I set out for them a pair of tattered cushions from which bits of cotton stuffing protrude.

"The tatami's soiled, so please use these, such as they are." I kneel down facing them again and greet them more formally. "I'm pleased to make your acquaintance. It seems that my husband has caused you a great deal of trouble. I have no idea what took place this evening, but I can't apologize enough for the frightful way he behaved just now. You see the sort of person he is . . ."

That's as far as I get before the tears start falling.

"Missus, forgive me, but may I ask how old you are?"

The man sits down on the torn cushion with no show of distaste. He crosses his legs and leans forward, resting his elbow on one knee and propping up his chin with his fist.

"My age?"

"Your husband's thirty, if I'm not mistaken?"

"That's right. And I'm, well, four years younger."

"Twenty-six? Unbelievable. I mean, that's about right, I suppose, if he's thirty, but still, it's a little surprising."

"I was thinking the same thing," the woman says, peering out from behind the man. "With a splendid young wife like this at home, why would he act the way he does?"

"He's sick, is what it is," the man says. "Sick. It wasn't so bad before, but he's been getting worse and worse."

He lets out a big sigh before carrying on in more solemn tones.

"The truth is, Missus, me and my wife here, we run a little restaurant bar near Nakano Station now, but we're both from the sticks. I did my best to earn an honest living as a shopkeeper back home, but eventually I got fed up haggling with cheapskate farmers, and since I guess you could say I always appreciated a little fun and excitement in life, some twenty years ago I dragged my wife here to Tokyo.

"We got a position as live-in helpers at a restaurant in Asakusa, and, well, after all the usual struggles, all the usual ups and downs, we finally got some savings together, and in 1936, I think it was, we rented a shack in Nakano – just one six-mat room with a small dirt-floor space in the front – and that's where we opened our humble little food-and-drinks place. It was the type of joint where the customers never had more than a yen or two to squander, but even so, by keeping our noses to the grindstone and denying ourselves any luxuries, we were able to accumulate a pretty good stockpile of gin and *shochu* and what have you, so that even when the shortages hit, we managed to keep going and not close up shop like so many did.

"Thanks to which, a lot of our more loyal customers started really pulling for us, and one of them even paved the way for us to gain access, little by little, to the sorts of liquor and delicacies that only people in the military or government could get their hands on back then. Then came the war with America and England, but even as the air raids got more and more intense, we didn't have any desire to evacuate to our hometown. Having no kids to worry about, we just clung to this one thing, our little shop, and told ourselves we'd stick with it until it burned to the ground. It was quite a relief when the war finally ended and our place was still standing. That's when we started openly stocking black-market liquor to sell, and . . .

"Well, that's basically our story. Of course, that's only the short version, and I suppose it might sound to you as if we haven't really had it so bad, that we've been relatively lucky, but I'll tell you what, Missus: life in this world is hell. They say there's little good and much evil in this world, and it's really true. With every ounce of happiness comes a pound of devilry. A man's lucky to have a single day free of worry – or even half a day – out of three hundred and sixty-five.

"It was in 1944 that your husband first came to our shop. It was spring, if I remember right, and the war hadn't yet become a lost cause – or, well, maybe we were already beaten, but nobody knew the reality of the situation, so to speak, the truth about what was going on. We all assumed that somehow, if we only stayed the course for two or three more years, we'd be able to reach some kind of equitable peace.

"As I recall, when he first came to our shop, your husband was wearing that inverness of his over a casual kimono. Not that such a style of dress was so unusual at the time. You rarely saw anybody wearing the bulky air-raid gear we all got used to later on, and lots of people were still strolling around town in regular civilian clothing, so it's not as if we looked down on him for that, or thought one way or the other about it, really. Anyway, he wasn't alone that night.

"I don't like to say it in front of you, Missus, but we're being frank here, and it's better not to hold anything back. A certain somewhat older woman had brought your husband to our place and slipped in with him through the rear entrance. At the time, see, like so many shops, we kept the front door locked but let a few regular customers enter discreetly through the back. In other words, we were 'closed for business,' as a popular phrase had it in those days. We didn't use the front room, where the tables and chairs are, but hosted people in the six-mat room in back, keeping the lights dim and our voices low – everyone getting quietly sloshed.

"This woman was a regular, who until recently had been working as a hostess at a bar in Shinjuku. So she was in the so-called water trade just like us, and she used to bring some pretty high-class clients to our place. Her apartment was nearby, and even after her bar had folded and she stopped hostessing, she'd drop in from time to time with male acquaintances. Well, once our stock of liquor started decreasing, we weren't all that grateful even for the best new customers – in fact, we almost began to resent them – but over the previous four or five years, she had shown up with a lot of folks who threw their money around pretty freely, so we felt we owed her a debt of gratitude and always welcomed her companions, serving them all with a smile.

"So when this woman – her name is Aki – when she led your husband in through the kitchen, we weren't particularly wary of him but just sat them down in the back room and got out the shochu. He was very subdued as he drank, and after Aki paid the bill, they left, again through the rear door. It's funny, but I can't forget how reserved and refined Ohtani seemed that night. Maybe that's always the form the devil takes when he first appears in your home – as a humble, innocent sort.

"Anyway, he seemed to take a liking to our place, and about ten days later he came back alone. He smiled sort of sheepishly and pressed a hundred-yen bill in my hand – which was still a lot of money back then, maybe equal to two or three thousand today, if not more. It looked as though he'd already had a few drinks somewhere, but as I'm sure you know, Missus, nobody can put it away like that man. Just when you think he must be three sheets to the wind, he'll suddenly turn serious and say something perfectly reasonable and articulate. I have never seen him stumble or stagger, either, no matter how much he drinks. It's true that a man of that age is at his prime when it comes to holding his liquor, but his is an extreme case.

"That night, too, as I said, he appeared to have drunk a fair amount somewhere else, and then at our place he had ten glasses of shochu, one right after the other, and hardly said anything the whole time. Even when my wife and I spoke to him, all he'd do is smile shyly, or nod in a vague sort of way, saying, 'Mm-hm, mm-hm.' And then suddenly he asks what time it is and jumps up to leave. I said, 'What about your change?' and he says, 'Keep it.' I told him I couldn't possibly do that, but he just grinned at me. 'Hang onto it till next time, then,' he said. 'I'll be back.'

"Well, Missus, that night was the first and last time we

ever got any money out of that man. From then on, he gave us one excuse after another, and in three years – while practically drinking us dry all by himself – he hasn't forked over a penny. What do you do with a person like that?"

I have no idea why, but this last remark makes me giggle. I hastily cover my mouth and glance at the man's wife, and she too suppresses a laugh and bows her head. And then even her husband breaks down and smiles wryly.

"It's no laughing matter, believe me, but sometimes you can get so fed up you almost feel like laughing. I'll tell you, a man of your husband's talents, if he made good use of them, he could become a Cabinet minister or a great scientist, or anything else he put his mind to. But my wife and I aren't the only ones to be taken in by him and then left in the lurch. That same Aki, for example, as a result of getting involved with Ohtani, lost her best patrons and ended up with nothing but the clothes on her back. Now she's living like a beggar in some filthy little room in the tenements.

"And yet, when she first met your husband, it was almost disgraceful how dizzy with excitement she was, and the way she raved about him. First of all, she said, his family background was spectacular. He was the second son of one Baron Ohtani, she said, and belonged to the family line of some feudal lord in Shikoku. And though he'd been disowned for misconduct, as soon as his father died he was going to split the estate with his elder brother and inherit a fortune.

"He was brilliant too, Aki told us, a true genius. When he was twenty-one, he published a book of poems that was even better than anything the great Ishikawa Takuboku ever wrote. He now had more than a dozen books under his belt, and in spite of his youth, he was considered Japan's greatest living poet. She told us that after attending the Peers School and First Higher School, Ohtani had gone on to graduate from the Imperial University, and that he was a regular wizard at German and French, and on and on – to hear Aki tell it, Ohtani was practically a god.

"Apparently, it wasn't just a pack of lies either. Other people too said he was a famous poet and the son of a baron, and even my old woman here gave Aki a run for her money when it came to going all gaga over the man. She'd say things like, 'There's just something different about people who've had a genteel upbringing,' and she was always looking forward to the great sensei's next visit. Pathetic. Nowadays, I guess, the nobility aren't what they used to be, but even so, up until the war ended, there was no better way to seduce women than to use the 'disinherited scion of the aristocracy' line. It seemed to drive the ladies wild.

"I guess that's the old 'slave mentality,' to use a phrase you hear a lot these days. Me, I'm just a man, and a pretty thick-skinned one at that, but as far as I'm concerned, there's no difference at all between people like us and the second son of a branch family of some aristocratic bigwig from the sticks. Pardon me, Missus, but that's the way I feel. I'm not about to get all weak-kneed over somebody like that, but I have to admit that your husband somehow had my number too. I'd tell myself that next time, no matter what he said, I wasn't going to serve him any more drinks, but then when I least expected it, he'd slip through the door, looking like a hunted man who'd finally found shelter. My resolve would waver, and the next thing I knew, I'd be pouring the liquor.

"He never got boisterous or anything, even when he was drunk, and really, if he'd only paid his bill, he would have been the perfect customer. He himself never bragged about his family background or called himself a genius or any of that nonsense, and if Aki was sitting next to him extolling his virtues, he'd derail the conversation by saying something totally unrelated. And every now and then he'd say, 'I just wish I had some cash. I'd really like to pay my tab here.'

"Well, he never did come up with any money; but sometimes Aki would pay for him, and then there was another woman, a married woman apparently, that he didn't seem to want Aki to know about but who he'd show up with from time to time, and she too would often chip in a little extra.

Otherwise, well, we're operating a business after all, and not in any position to let anyone go on drinking for free forever – whether it's the great Ohtani-sensei or an Imperial prince. Mind you, those occasional little payments from his companions didn't even come close to squaring things. We're running a massive loss on this man.

"We had heard that he was married and had a house in Koganei, and I thought I'd call on him privately sometime to discuss the situation. So one night I asked him what part of town he lived in, trying to be casual about it, but he read me like a book and said, 'Can't give you what I don't have. Why are you always fretting about things like this? Nobody wins when friends turn into enemies.' He was quick to say unpleasant things like that, but it didn't stop me from wanting to find out where he lived. I even tried following him home two or three times, but he always managed to give me the slip.

"Then the heavy bombing started here in Tokyo, and in those days, bizarre as it might sound, Ohtani would come barging into our place wearing an army field cap, open the cupboard himself, pull out a bottle of brandy or something, help himself to a few slugs without even sitting down, and then fly out the door like a gust of wind. No payment, no anything.

"When the war ended, even shops like ours were able to openly stock black-market liquor. We hung a brand-new *noren* curtain out front, and really gave it our all. We were still small and still struggling, but we hired a girl to help out and to appeal to customers. And then that demon sensei reared his head again.

"He would show up not with women but with two or three newspaper or magazine reporters. According to some of these fellows, now that the military had fallen, the impoverished poets and artists were going to be the new popular heroes. They'd proclaim things like that, and Ohtani-sensei would give some kind of baffling response, with all sort of words that I couldn't tell you if they were foreigners' names or English phrases or philosophical terms or what. But then suddenly he'd jump up out of his seat and slip outside. And that would be the last we'd see of him. After a while it would begin to dawn on the reporters that he'd left – 'Where the hell'd he go?' Eventually they'd start getting ready to leave, and I'd have to say, 'Just a moment, gentlemen. Sensei pulls stunts like this all the time. I'll need you to settle the bill.' Sometimes they'd split the bill among themselves and meekly go on their way, but some got angry and shouted at me. 'Make Ohtani pay! We have to live on five hundred yen a month!' But I'd stand my ground and say, 'Do you have any idea how much that man already owes me? I'll tell you what,' I'd say. 'If you fellows can get him to pay back any fraction of that debt, I'll split it with you fifty-fifty.

"Some of them looked pretty disgusted after hearing that. 'Well, I'll be damned,' they'd grumble. 'I didn't realize Ohtani was such a rat. Won't be drinking with him again.' Then one of them would turn to me and say, 'I'm afraid we don't have a hundred yen between us tonight, sir. I'll bring the money tomorrow.' And he'd whip off his overcoat and hand it to me, saying, 'Here, hold on to this until then.' You always hear that reporters are a low class of people, but if that's so, then why is it that they're so much more honest and upstanding the the noble sensei himself? If Ohtani's the second son of a baron, then the reporters he brought here must be the first sons of dukes or something.

"After the war, he started drinking even more, always with this grim, severe expression on his face. He started telling vulgar jokes too, something he'd never done before, and sometimes he'd actually punch a reporter, or start a shoving match. And then, at some point, it came to our attention that he had seduced the girl we'd hired, who wasn't even twenty at the time. That really shocked us, and put us in a very difficult situation. But what's done is done, and we knew we had no choice but to live with the shame of it. We told the girl to give up any silly illusions she might have, and we quietly sent her back to her folks.

"At that point I pleaded with him. I said, 'Ohtani-san, I'm not going to say anything about all this. But I beg you, please don't come here anymore.' And how does he respond to that? He threatens me! 'For somebody raking it in on the black market, you're a real model of morality, eh? I know all about your operation, you know.' He says it like that, like some kind of underworld thug. And the very next night, here he comes again, as casual as can be. At our shop, we've been dealing in the black market since during the war, and maybe now we're paying for it by having to deal with this monster of a man. But, I mean, if he's capable of doing the sort of thing he did tonight, well ... To me he's not a poet or a sensei or anything but a common thief. He stole five thousand yen from our house tonight, Missus.

"Most of our money goes to staying well stocked, so we usually don't have more than five hundred or a thousand yen in the house. And that's the truth. Whatever money we get in sales goes straight to suppliers. But tonight, the reason we had that five thousand yen is, what with New Year's being almost upon us, I had been going around to customers' houses, asking them to settle their bills, and had finally managed to scrounge together that much. And if we don't hand this exact amount to our creditors tonight, well, in the new year we won't be able to go on as a business – that's how important that money is to us. My wife was counting it in the back room, and Ohtani was drinking by himself at a table in the front. He must've seen her put the money in the cabinet drawer, because suddenly he shoots up from his seat and heads straight back there. He nudges my wife aside, opens the drawer, snatches up that five-thousand-yen bundle, stuffs it in his pocket, and before we even know what's happening, he's in the front room again and out through the door.

"I yelled something at the top of my lungs, and we both chased after him, my wife and I. At this point I was just about ready to start shouting 'Thief!' so that people on the street would tackle him. But Ohtani's a regular visitor after all, and the last thing a business like ours needs is a scandal. So we decided to follow him and not let him out of our sight this time, no matter what, until we tracked him to a place where we could talk things over calmly and get him to return the money. By working as a team, my wife and I finally succeeded in finding your house, so here we come, stifling our anger and politely asking him to give back what he took, and what happens? He pulls out a knife and threatens to stab me! I mean, what the hell?"

Once again, for reasons I don't understand, I find myself laughing out loud. The man's wife blushes and chuckles a little too, but I can't stop. I don't mean any disrespect to the man, but there's something strangely comical about the way he tells his story, and I laugh until I'm literally in tears. For a moment I wonder if this isn't what my husband was talking about in one of his poems: "The roar of laughter at civilization's end."

2.

In any case, laughter isn't going to solve this problem. I have to think of something, but all I can really offer is my word. "I'm going to make this right," I tell them. "Please wait for just one more day before notifying the police." I ask for directions to their place, solemnly promising to call on them tomorrow. Finally they give in to my heartfelt plea, and we say goodbye for the time being. Once they're gone, I sit down alone in the center of the cold room and wonder what to do. Not a single good plan comes to me, however, and at last I get up and take off my wrap and crawl under the covers of the boy's futon. I lie here stroking his head and hoping that dawn will never break.

My father used to run a little stand in Asakusa Park, a wheeled cart where he cooked and sold oden. My mother died when I was little. My father and I lived in the tenements, and I worked alongside him at the stand. That's where I met Ohtani. He would stop by from time to time, and eventually I started meeting him at other places too, secretly. Before very long, I was pregnant with the boy, and after a lot of fuss and confusion, Ohtani and I began living together as man and wife. Of course, I'm not in his family register or anything, which means that the boy is technically fatherless.

Sometimes Ohtani leaves the house and doesn't come back for two or three nights. Other times it might be a month. I don't know where he goes or what he does, but when he returns he's always drunk, pale as a ghost, and breathing laboriously. He'll gaze at my face, and sometimes tears will run down his cheeks. Sometimes he'll crawl into my futon, shaking life a leaf, and hold me tight and whimper things like, "I can't take it anymore. I'm scared. I'm so scared. Please help me!" And sometimes he'll talk deliriously in his sleep, moaning and groaning. And then, the following day, he'll be in a sort of daze, like a man whose soul has been stolen, and before I know it, he's off again and doesn't come back for several more nights. Fortunately, he has two or three old acquaintances in the publishing business who are kind enough to worry about the boy and me, and occasionally they bring us a little money. So far, at least, we've managed to avoid starving to death.

I doze off, and when I open my eyes, rays of morning light are piercing the cracks in the shutters. I get up and dress, then strap the boy to my back and leave the house. I couldn't possibly sit quietly at home doing nothing.

With no particular destination in mind, I make my way toward the train station. I buy a hard candy at a stand next to the station and give it to the boy to suck on. And suddenly it's clear to me where I need to go. First I buy a ticket for Kichijoji. Once I'm on the train, hanging on to a hand strap, I look up vacantly at one of the ads suspended from the ceiling and notice my husband's name. It's an advertisement for a magazine to which he's contributed a long article titled "François Villon." For reasons I don't understand, as I'm standing there looking up at that title and my husband's name below it, bitter tears well up and the words go all blurry.

I get off at Kichijoji Station and decide to stroll through Inokashira Park, for the first time in I don't know how many years. All of the cedar trees around the pond have been chopped down. It looks so bleak, so bare and exposed, like a construction site or something. So different from the way it used to be.

I unstrap the boy, and we sit side by side on a half-collapsed bench near the pond. I feed him a roasted sweet potato I brought from home.

"See the pretty pond? Once there were lots and lots of koi-koi and goldfishies in the water. Now, no fishies at all. Too bad!"

I don't know what the boy makes of this, but he looks up at me, his cheeks stuffed with sweet potato, and laughs in an odd way: "Keh! Keh!"

He's my son, my baby, but I'm afraid he's essentially an idiot.

We sit there looking at the pond for a while, but I realize I'm not going to find any answers here, so eventually I get up, strap the boy to my back again, and wander back the way we came. I stroll through the bustling shopping area, taking in all the sights, and when I reach the station, I buy a ticket for Nakano. I have no plan of action, no ideas whatsoever, and even as I step aboard the train, I feel as if I'm being sucked into some sort of hellish abyss. The train deposits me at Nakano Station. I wind my way through the streets, following the directions I was given yesterday, and soon I'm standing in front of the couple's little restaurant bar. The sign above the door says The Camellias.

The front entrance is locked, so I walk around to the kitchen door. The madam is in the shop alone, tidying up. As soon as our eyes meet, I blurt out a lie that takes even me by surprise.

"Good news! I'll be able to pay you back in full this evening, or by tomorrow at the latest. I found a way, and it's all arranged now, so please set your mind at ease."

"Oh my, that is good news," she says, and her face brightens a little. But I see shadows of doubt there too.

"No, really! A certain person is going to bring the money here, right to the shop. Without fail. And I'll be your hostage until the cash arrives. How's that for a guarantee? In the meantime, I can help you out in the shop!"

I unstrap the boy and set him down in the back room to play by himself, then begin bustling about, eager to show how helpful I can be. The boy's used to playing alone, and he's no bother at all. It may be that he's simply too dimwitted to be wary of strangers, but he has nothing but smiles for the madam. When she sends me out to collect their weekly ration of rice, she gives him a tin of American canned goods to play with, and he amuses himself the entire time tapping on it and rolling it on the floor.

It's about noon when the boss returns with fresh fish and vegetables for the shop. As soon as I seem him, I blurt out the same lie I told his wife. He gives me a quizzical look.

"Is that so? Well, Missus, you know, money is something you can't count on until you're holding it in your hand." He says this in a surprisingly gentle but worldly-wise sort of way.

"No," I tell him, "it really is for certain. Please trust me on this, and do give me until tomorrow before you go bringing charges. Meanwhile, I can help out around the shop!"

"Well, as long as we get the money back ... After all, the end of the year is only five or six days away now."

"Yes. That's why I – Oh, we have customers. Welcome!"

I beam at the three workmen who've entered the shop, and whisper to the madam, "Can you led me an apron?"

"Whoa!" says one of the men. "You went and hired yourself a beauty queen, did you?"

"And don't you be trying to seduce her," says the boss, in a tone that suggests he's not merely kidding. "We've got a lot of money riding on this one."

"One of those million-dollar thoroughbreds, is she?"

As I heat the sake, I respond to this rather vulgar remark in kind. "Even among thoroughbreds," I tell them, "they say that fillies only cost half as much."

"Don't sell yourself short!" the youngest of the workmen shouts. "From now on in Japan, it's all about equality of the sexes, whether you're a horse or a dog or anything else. Seriously, though, Miss," he says, "I'm in love. It's love at first sight. But, wait – you've got a kid?"

"It's not hers," says the madam, stepping in from the back room with the boy in her arms. "This child was left to us by relatives. We've finally got an heir to take over the shop."

"It's a big money business, after all," one of the men says, teasing her, but the boss doesn't look amused.

"With a little monkey business thrown in," he mutters. "Monkey business and debts." Then he abruptly switches to his hearty shopkeeper's voice. "So, what'll it be? Shall we prepare a big stew?"

I've just learned something. *I knew it*, I'm thinking, and nod to myself. But I act as if nothing has happened as I bring the men their sake.

Apparently tonight is what's known as Christmas Eve, which may be why the customers keep pouring in. I've hardly eaten a thing all day, but I'm so full of anguish that even when the madam urges me to grab a bite, I tell her I'm stuffed and couldn't possibly. I just continue flitting about like a frantic butterfly, and though it may be mere vanity on my part, I get the impression that my presence adds a bit of color and vitality to the place. More than a few of the customers ask my name and want to shake my hand.

But what's going to come of all this? I have no idea. I smile and respond to the customers' lewd jokes with equally risqué wisecracks as I slip from one to another, filling their cups, all the while wishing I could simply melt away, like ice cream.

But sometimes miracles really do occur in this world.

It's a little past nine in the evening when it happens. A man comes in wearing a black half mask, like the one worn by the gentleman burglar Lupin, and a three-cornered paper party hat. He's accompanied by a willowy and very pretty woman in her midthirties. The man sits down with his back to me on a chair in one corner of the front room, but I knew who he was the moment he came in. My husband, the thief. He, for his part, hasn't noticed me. I don't let on but continue joking around with the other customers until the slender woman, who sits facing my husband, calls to me.

"Excuse me, Miss?"

"Yes, ma'am," I say, and make my way to their table. "Welcome! What can I bring you to drink?"

My husband looks up at me through the eyeholes of his mask. He looks surprised, understandably enough, but all I do is pat him on the shoulder and say, "Congratulations on Christmas! Is that the right expression? You look like you could handle another bottle or two."

The woman doesn't reply to that but gives me a serious look and says, "There's something I'd like to discuss privately with the owner of the shop. Could you ask him to join us for a moment?"

I find the boss in the back room, deep-frying something.

"My husband is here," I tell him, "and he'd like to speak with you. But please don't say anything about me in front of the woman he's with. I don't want to embarrass him."

"He finally showed up, did he?"

I know the boss doubted my tale about the money at first, but maybe I've gained his trust. He must assume I'm responsible for my husband's arrival.

"Don't say anything about me," I remind him as he heads for the front room.

"If you'd rather I don't, I won't," he says cheerfully.

After quickly surveying the room, he walks straight to my husband's table. He exchanges a few words with the pretty woman, and then the three of them stand up and leave the shop together.

All is well now. I find myself truly believing that everything's been resolved, and I can't help but feel exhilarated. I seize the wrist of a young customer in a dark-blue kimono with white splash patterns, a boy of no more than twenty.

"Drink up! Let's drink! It's Christmas!"

### 3.

About half an hour later, or even less – much sooner than I expected, at any rate – the boss returns alone and walks right up to me.

"Thank you, Missus. I got the money back."

"Oh, good! All of it?"

He gives me a funny smile.

"Well, just the amount taken last night, but …"

"How much is it altogether? Approximately, I mean. Giving us your most generous discount."

"Twenty thousand yen."

"That's all?"

"My most generous discount."

"I'll return it in full. Will you hire me here, starting tomorrow? Please? I'll work it all off."

"Missus, you're quite the ministering angel, aren't you?" he says, and we both laugh.

Sometime after ten, I strap the boy to my back and return to our home in Koganei. My husband isn't here, but I'm not bothered. Tomorrow I'll be back at the shop, and maybe I'll see him there. I wonder why I didn't think of this in the first place. I only agonized so much because

I was too stupid to see the obvious answer. I was always good at dealing with customers when I was helping at my father's oden stand, and I know I'll get on well at the place in Nakano. Tonight, in fact, I earned almost five hundred yen in tips.

According to the story the boss pieced together, my husband ran off to a friend's house last night and stayed there till this morning. He then went to a bar in Kyobashi that's owned by the pretty woman he was with tonight, and there he started drinking whiskey and handing out "Christmas presents," as he called them, in the form of wads of cash, to the five girls who work there. At around noon, he summoned a taxi and went off somewhere, coming back a short time later with his mask and paper hat, a decorated cake, and a whole roasted turkey. He then proceeded to telephone all over town, inviting acquaintances to his feast. The madam of the bar, knowing that Ohtani never had any money, naturally grew suspicious, and when she privately questioned him, he calmly told her all about what he'd done the night before. Obviously, he and she were no strangers to begin with, but in any case he confided in her, saying that if he didn't return the money, the police might get involved and things could turn ugly. She offered to cover the debt, and asked my husband to take her to the restaurant bar in Nakano.

"That's about what I imagined he'd do with the cash he

stole, but you had that worked out pretty well, didn't you, Missus? Did you ask a friend of his for help or something?"

Sure enough, the boss is convinced I expected this to happen. I just smile and say, "What else could I do?"

My life has changed completely now. It's been transformed into something full of joy and light. The following day, I went straight to a salon and had my hair done. I've also put together a little cosmetics kit and resewn my kimono, and the madam gave me two new pairs of white *tabi* socks. I feel as if all the heavy, painful feelings in my heart have been washed clean away.

I get up each morning, eat breakfast with the boy, pack a lunch, strap him to my back, and head to work in Nakano. New Year's is a busy time for the shop, and Sat-chan of the Camellias, as they call me here, has been as busy as a bee. My husband drops in every other night or so. He lets me pay his bill and then vanishes like the wind, but later he'll often poke his head in the door and say, "You ready to go?" I nod and gather my things, and we enjoy a pleasant trip home together.

"Why haven't I been doing this all along? I'm so happy now."

"There is no happiness or unhappiness for women," he tells me.

"Oh? Well, you may be right, for all I know. What about men?"

"A man knows only unhappiness. He's forever battling the horror of it all."

"That's too deep for me. But I for one would like to go on living like this. The owner of the Camellias and his wife are such good people."

"They're fools, is what they are – a pair of stupid hicks. And avaricious. They get me to drink and then try to profit from it."

"That's called running a business. It's only natural. But I think there's more to it than that. You fooled around with the madam, didn't you?"

"A long time ago. Why? Does the old man suspect anything?"

"Apparently. I once heard him say something about 'monkey business and debts.'"

"Listen. I know how affected this sounds, but . . . I want to die so bad I can't stand it. From the time I was born, all I've ever thought about is dying. It would be better for everybody if I did – that's clear enough. But I can't seem to do it. Some strange kind of, terrifying kind of god keeps stopping me."

"That's because you have your work to do."

"My work means nothing. I have no masterpieces and no spectacular flops. If people say a piece is good, it's good, and if they say it stinks, it stinks. It's exactly like breathing in and breathing out – inspiration and expiration. What scares me is that, somewhere in our world, there is a God. There really is one, right?"

"Huh?"

"There is a God, right?"

"I have no idea."

"Oh."

After almost three weeks of commuting each day to the Camellias, I've come to realize something about the customers. Every single one of them is a criminal of some sort. In fact, my husband may be one of the more benign ones. It's not only the customers either. I've begun to think that everyone I see on the street is harboring some sort of dark and terrible secret.

An elegantly dressed woman in her fifties comes to the rear door of the shop to sell bottles of sake at three hundred yen apiece. That's well below market price, so the madam snatches them up, but it turns out the sake is watered down. In a world where even a refined lady like that has to stoop to such schemes, maybe it's impossible to survive without having a dark side. Is it possible that morality in this world is like that game where a card counts against you unless you can push it on someone else?

God, if you do exist, show yourself!

At the end of the New Year's season, a customer will violate me.

It's a rainy night. My husband hasn't shown his face, but Yajima-san, an acquaintance of his from the publishing company, is here with a colleague, another man in his midforties. They're loudly carrying on, jokingly debating whether it's a good thing or a bad thing that Ohtani's wife is working in a bar. I laugh and join in, saying, "And where is this wife of his?"

"Beats me," says Yajima. "But I'll bet you she's a lot more elegant and beautiful than Sat-chan of the Camellias."

"Oh, I'm so jealous," I shoot right back. "I'd love to spend even one night with someone like Ohtani-san. I'm mad about devious devils like that."

Yajima-san makes a sour face and turns to his friend. "You see how it is?" he says.

By now, all the reporters Ohtani brings to the bar know that I'm his wife, and an assortment of odd characters who've also caught wind of this come here to test and tease me. The bar gets busier and livelier by the day, and the boss is in better spirits than ever.

Yajima-san and his friend go on to discuss some business deal involving black-market paper, and then, at a little past ten, they leave.

Rain is still falling, and it seems my husband won't be making an appearance, so even though one customer is still here, I collect my things and pick up the boy, who's been sleeping in the back room. When I ask the madam if I can borrow an umbrella, the customer speaks up.

"I've got an umbrella. I'll escort you home."

He's a small, thin man of twenty-five or so who looks like a factory worker. I've never seen him here before. He stands up with a serious look on his face.

"That's very kind of you, but I'm used to commuting alone."

"You live in Koganei, right? I'm in the same neighborhood. I'll be glad to see you home. Check please, ma'am."

He's only had three drinks and doesn't seem especially intoxicated.

We board the train and get off at Koganei, then walk side by side through the dark streets, sharing the umbrella. He hasn't said much the whole time, but as we near my house, he comes out with a series of clipped remarks.

"I know who your husband is. I'm a fan of Ohtani-sensei's poetry. I write poems too, you see. I was hoping to have him read my stuff. I'm a bit intimidated by him, though."

When we reach my door, I thank him and say, "I'm sure we'll meet again at the Camellias."

"Yes. Good night," he says, and walks off in the rain.

I'm awakened in the middle of the night by the front door clattering open, but I assume it's only my husband coming home drunk again. I just lie here quietly. Then I hear a man's voice.

"Excuse me! Ohtani-san? Excuse me."

I get up, turn on the light, and go to the entrance. The

same young man is there, so drunk he can barely stand.

"Forgive me, Missus. I stopped off for another drink on the way home. Truth is, my house is in Tachikawa, but when I got to the station, no more trains! Missus, can I ask you a favor? Could you let me stay here tonight? I don't need a futon or anything. Right here in the entryway is fine. If I could only catch a few winks, until the first train in the morning ... I'd sleep outside somewhere, but the rain is really coming down."

"My husband isn't home, but ... Well, if you really don't mind sleeping in the entrance here ..."

I bring him a couple of our tattered cushions and lay them on the step above the entryway.

"Thanks. Ah, I'm so drunk," he says, in a small, pained voice, and flops right down on the cushions. By the time I get back to my room, he's already snoring loudly.

And then, at dawn the next morning, he makes short work of forcing himself on me.

Later I strap the boy to my back and commute to the Camellias as always, maintaining a casual demeanor, as if nothing has happened.

When I get to the shop, I find my husband sitting alone at a table with a glass of liquor, reading a newspaper. The morning light illuminates the glass, and I'm struck by how pretty it looks.

"Isn't anyone here?"

He turns and looks at me. "Hmm. The old man went

out to pick up supplies. The old woman was in the kitchen awhile ago. Is she gone too?"

"You didn't show up here last night."

"Sure I did. Lately I can't get to sleep unless I've seen my favorite waitress's face. It was after ten, though, and they told me you'd just left for home."

"And?"

"I spent the night here. It was raining like hell."

"Maybe I should ask if I can move in here myself."

"Not a bad idea."

"I'll do it. No sense in renting that house forever."

He doesn't reply to this but turns his eyes back to the newspaper.

"Well, they're vilifying me in the press again. They're calling me a hedonist and a pseudoaristocrat. That's not even accurate. They should say something like, 'He's a hedonist who lives in terror of God.' Look at this right here, Sat-chan. It says I'm a fiend. That's not true, is it? I don't mind telling you now, the only reason I took that five thousand yen was because I wanted to treat you and the boy to a nice New Year's for once. Would a fiend do something like that?"

I'm not particularly happy to hear this.

"Never mind," I tell him. "Even being a fiend is all right. As long as we can go on living – that's all that really matters."

# OSAN

### I.

He slips out the front door on silent feet, like a man whose soul has been removed. I'm in the kitchen cleaning up after dinner but I sense him leaving. It makes me so sad I almost drop the dish in my hand, and a sigh escapes my lips as I stand on tiptoe to look out the latticed window and see, on the little path next to the hedge that's all entangled with pumpkin tendrils, my husband, walking away in his wash-worn white yukata with a thin band tied around the waist, seeming to float in the summer twilight like a ghost, like something that doesn't belong in this world, like misery and sorrow incarnate.

"Where's Papa going?"

Our seven-year-old daughter, who was playing outside, innocently asks me this as she washes her feet with water from the bucket outside the kitchen door. This child is much more attached to her father than to me; each night they lay out their futons side by side, under the same mosquito netting.

"To the temple."

I say this without thinking but immediately regret, with a chill, what feels like an ill omen.

"The temple? Why?"

"It's O-Bon season, right? To pay his respects to the ancestors."

The lies roll out easily, oddly enough. It really is the thirteenth day of O-Bon, however. Little girls at other houses are playing outside their front gates, proudly waving and flapping the long sleeves of their pretty kimonos, but our children's good clothing all went up in flames during the war, and now, O-Bon or not, they have nothing but shabby Western-style clothes to wear.

"Oh. Will he be back soon?"

"Well, I wonder. If you're good, Masako, maybe he'll be back before you know it."

That's what I tell her, but judging by the way he left, I know he'll be sleeping elsewhere tonight.

Masako steps up into the kitchen, then into the three-mat room, where she sits gazing out the window and looking forlorn.

"Mama, look! Masako's bean plants have flowers now."

Her quiet exclamation touches me to the quick, and tears fill my eyes as I trot to the window.

"Let me see! Yes, you're right. That means the beans will be forming soon."

Adjoining our front door is a small plot of land, roughly twenty by twenty feet, where I used to grow various kinds of vegetables, but with three children now I just don't have time for tending a garden, and my husband, who used to lend a hand on occasion, no longer helps out at all around the house. The garden next door, thanks to the man who lives there, is beautifully maintained and produces all manner of fresh produce, while ours, shamefully, is overgrown with weeds. But Masako took a single bean from our rations, buried it in the dirt nearest the house and watered it, and before long a sprout burst forth. That bean sprout became my toyless firstborn's one and only treasure, and she proudly boasts, "You should see my beanstalk!" to anyone who'll listen.

Ruin. Misery. In today's Japan, it's not only our family to which such words pertain, especially here in Tokyo, where everyone you see seems beaten down and defeated, moving sluggishly about, as if against their will. We too lost all our possessions to the firebombs and have any number of reasons to think of ourselves as ruined, but what's truly painful for me now has nothing to do with such material matters. I struggle, rather, with an even more pressing issue, as the wife of a man in this world.

My husband has been working for a well-known magazine publisher in Kanda for nearly ten years. Eight years ago, he and I were joined in a normal arranged marriage. Tokyo rents were already getting expensive at the time, so we found a small house on farmland outside the city but near the Chuo Line, and we lived here until the war.

Because my husband is physically infirm he avoided being drafted or conscripted and continued to commute to his office each day. But once the bombing raids intensified and the airplane production plant and other strategic facilities around our town were targeted, bombs frequently rained down near our house, and finally one of them exploded in the bamboo grove right behind us, destroying the kitchen, the toilet, and the three-mat room. Masako's baby brother Yoshitaro had just been born, and it wasn't possible for the four of us to carry on living in the half-ruined house, so I took the two children and evacuated to my hometown in Aomori. My husband stayed on here alone, sleeping in the six-mat room and still commuting to work each day.

Less than four months after we evacuated, however, Aomori too was hit by air raids and more or less burned to the ground. All the belongings we'd struggled so hard to bring with us went up in smoke, leaving us with literally nothing but the clothes on our backs. We took refuge in the unburned home of an acquaintance, where I, utterly at a loss and driven half-mad by our wretched situation, learned what hell must be like. We burdened these people with our presence for about ten days, and then came the news of Japan's unconditional surrender. Eager to return to Tokyo and my husband, I hurried back with the two children, and we arrived looking like a trio of street beggars. Having no other place to move into, we hired a carpenter to do rough repairs on our half-destroyed house, and the four of us resumed life as a family, enjoying a brief respite from our troubles – at least until circumstances began to change for my husband.

The publishing company had been damaged in the bombings, and now some sort of fracas involving capital occurred among the top executives, as a result of which the company was dissolved and my husband found himself suddenly unemployed. Having spent years in publishing, however, he had many acquaintances in the business, and he ended up partnering with other prominent individuals in starting a new publishing company. The company began with moderate success, issuing two or three separate periodicals, but soon ran into difficulties obtaining paper, which proved fatal and led to a considerable loss. This left my husband deeply in debt and struggling to cope with the aftermath. He would leave the house each morning and return each evening looking exhausted. He had always been the quiet sort, but now he tended to clam up completely. Eventually he managed to pay off all his debt, but by then he'd lost the will or energy to work.

He can't just lie around house all day, however. He stands on the veranda smoking a cigarette and gazing out at the horizon, pondering heaven knows what, while I worry that it's starting up again, and then, sure enough, he lets out a defeated sigh, flicks his cigarette butt into the garden, retrieves the billfold from the desk drawer and shoves it into his pocket, and now I see him walking soundlessly away, like a man whose soul has been removed, and I can tell he probably won't be home tonight.

He's been a good husband, and kind. When it comes to drinking, he can barely finish a single cup of sake or bottle of beer, and though he smokes cigarettes, the rationed allotment is usually more than sufficient for him. We've been married ten years now, and he has never struck me, or even cursed at me. I can think of only one time when I feared him. He was meeting with an associate one day when Masako, who was only two at the time, toddled up to the visitor and accidentally knocked over his cup of tea. Apparently my husband called to me, but I was fanning the flames in the clay stove and didn't hear him. When I failed to respond, he burst into the kitchen with Masako in his arms and a look of absolute rage on his face, a look such as I've never seen before or since. He set Masako down on the wood flooring and said nothing but stood there for some moments, scowling and glaring at me with murderous eyes, before turning away and going back to the other room, slamming the sliding door shut so loudly that it seemed to vibrate in the marrow of my bones. I was left trembling for some time, shocked to see firsthand the potential brutality of the male. But that's the only time I remember him ever losing his temper with me. Like everyone else, I've seen my share of suffering as a result of the war, but when I think of my husband's kindness over these past eight years, I have to admit I feel very fortunate.

(He's become like a different person now, however. When did this start? When I saw him on our return to Tokyo, after four months in Aomori, I sensed something contrite in his smile, and he seemed almost timid, avoiding eye contact. I simply put it down to the discomfort and inconvenience he'd experienced fending for himself all that time, and my heart went out to him, but ... On the other hand, maybe during those four months ... No, I won't think about it. Thinking only leads to a quagmire of despair.)

Though I'm sure he won't be using it, I lay out my husband's futon next to Masako's and hang the mosquito netting, as pain and sorrow fill my heart.

2.

A little before noon the next day I'm at the well out front, washing Toshiko's diapers (Toshiko is our second daughter, born this spring), when my husband slips stealthily into the yard, looking as shifty as a thief, or a fugitive. As he passes in front of me, he gives a silent little bow of his head, and then trips and pitches forward through the open front door. The fact that he instinctively bowed, however slightly, to me, his wife, pierces my heart. I can't help pitying him, knowing that he too is suffering, and I can't go on just doing the laundry. I stand up and follow him into the house.

"It's awfully hot today. Why don't you get undressed? An O-Bon ration bonus of two bottles of beer was delivered today. I've got them on ice. How does that sound?"

He smiles timidly and says, "Great." His voice is weak and unusually husky. "How about if Mother and I drink together, a bottle each?"

It's a transparent and inept attempt to humor me.

"I'd be delighted," I tell him.

My late father was a big drinker, which may help explain why, though I rarely drink, my capacity for alcohol is actually greater than my husband's. Once, when we were still newlyweds, he and I were strolling through Shinjuku and stopped to eat oden noodles or something, with a cup of sake each. He face quickly turned bright red, and he got hopelessly tipsy, whereas I didn't feel anything at all, outside of a little unexplained ringing in my ears.

In the three-mat room, the children are eating lunch; my husband, stripped to a loincloth and with a wet hand towel draped over his shoulders, sips beer; I join him in only a cupful, not wanting to waste any, then sit cradling and breastfeeding Toshiko. On the surface, we're the very picture of a harmonious family unit, but inwardly everything feels awkward. My husband avoids meeting my eyes, and I, for my part, have to carefully choose my words so as not to touch on any subjects that might be painful for him. In other words, the conversation does not flow. Masako and Yoshitaro seem somehow to sense the tension between their parents and are being remarkably quiet and well-behaved as they dip their steamed bread meal substitute into cups of dulcin-sweetened tea.

"Whoa," he says. "Alcohol in the daytime hits pretty hard, doesn't it."

"Oh my, it's true – your face is bright red!"

As I'm saying this, I notice something. Just beneath my husband's chin, imprinted on his neck, is something that resembles a purple moth. And no, it's not a moth. I've seen these before, back when we were newly married, and when I catch a glimpse of this one my heart stops beating for a moment, even as my flustered husband seems to notice that I've noticed. He clumsily adjusts the wet hand towel to cover the bite mark, which tells me why the hand towel was there in the first place. But I make every effort to pretend I've noticed nothing.

"Masako, the bun-buns taste better when Papa's here, right?" It's meant to sound lighthearted, but now that I've said it, it hangs in the air like sarcasm, dampening the mood even more, and as my suffering increases, we suddenly hear the French national anthem start up on the radio at the house next door.

At the first notes, he mumbles to himself: "Oh, that's right. It's Bastille Day today." He cracks a faint smile, and then directs the following speech to both Masako and me.

"The fourteenth of July. This is the day that a revolution . . ."

His words break off suddenly, and I look up to see his lips oddly twisted and a misty glistening in his eyes. He seems to be trying to hold back tears as he continues, with a sob in his voice.

"The Bastille, you know, the prison, was stormed by the people. People came from all over France to rise up, you know, and they put an end, for all time, to the idle nobility's luxurious way of life. The aristocracy lost that life forever. But they *had* to be destroyed. Even though it was clear that the new morality, based on the new order, was doomed to failure, the aristocrats had to be destroyed.

It's said that just before his death, Sun Yat-sen declared that 'the revolution has not yet succeeded.' Maybe he was right. Maybe revolutions can never be completed. But even so, we must never stop trying. That's the true nature of revolution: it's heartbreakingly sad and breathtakingly beautiful. What does revolution bring us? Sadness and beauty, and love ..."

With the French national anthem still playing, my husband bursts into tears, and then, plainly embarrassed, tries to laugh it off.

"Whoops. I'm afraid Papa's just another maudlin drunk," he says, turning away. He stands up and goes to the kitchen, and while washing his face says, "Yeah, that wasn't good. Got too drunk. Weeping over the French Revolution, ha! I need a nap."

He goes into the six-mat room, and no more is heard from him, but I can picture him in there, curled up, holding himself, and stifling sobs.

He isn't weeping about revolution. Then again, perhaps the revolution in France is actually a good metaphor for an extramarital affair. The anguish of having to destroy France's romantic monarchy for the sake of something sad and beautiful, might be compared to the anguish my husband suffers in destroying a harmonious household. I understand that well enough. The problem is that I'm still in love with my husband. I'm not Osan from the old Chikamatsu play, but ...

*In the wife's bosom*
*Can it be a demon?*
*Fiery and fervent*
*Can it be a serpent?*

To talk of revolution and subversive ideology while brushing off your wife's alienation as irrelevant, leaving her alone and stuck and endlessly sighing – what can this lead to? Is she just to submit, entrusting her fate to heaven and praying for a change in the shifting winds of her husband's affections? I have three children. For their sake as well, I couldn't leave my husband now if I wanted to.

Whenever he's stayed elsewhere for two consecutive nights or so, even this husband of mine will make sure to spend an evening at home and sleep in his own futon. After dinner he plays with the children on the veranda, but his exchanges with them feel rote and empty. Lifting our newborn baby with clumsy hands, he coos, "Ooh, iddn't she chubby! Such a pwetty baby!"

And I, without meaning anything in particular, join in. "She's a cutie, all right. Looking at your children makes you want to live a long life, doesn't it?"

His expression changes instantly.

"Mm."

It pains him even to grunt this response. *Whoops*, I think, cold sweat escaping my pores.

Whenever my husband sleeps at home, he retires to the

six-mat room by eight o'clock; lays out his and Masako's futons; hangs the mosquito netting; changes Masako, who still wants to play with Papa, into her sleeping gown; tucks her in; gets under the covers himself; turns out the light; and that's it.

I lay the boy and the baby down in the four-and-a-half-mat room, then do my sewing work until eleven or so, when I hang the netting and lie down between the two little ones.

I can't sleep. It seems my husband in the next room can't sleep either; I hear him sigh, and I too sigh without intending to, and then I remember that singsong quote from Osan:

> *In the wife's bosom*
> *Can it be a demon?*
> *Fiery and fervent*
> *Can it be a serpent?*

And now my husband gets out of bed and comes into my room. I tense up, but all he says is: "Do we have any sleeping pills?"

"We did, but I took them last night. They didn't work anyway."

"That's what happens when you take too many. Six pills is just about right."

He does not sound happy.

3.

Day after day of oppressive heat. What with the stifling weather and all my worries, it's hard to get food down. My cheekbones have begun to protrude, and the breast-milk I feed my baby is down to a trickle. My husband too seems to have no appetite; his eyes are sunken, with a grim glister.

"It would be easier just to go insane," he says suddenly, with a derisive snort

"I feel the same way."

"People who live correctly shouldn't suffer. There's one thing I can't understand: How do you people manage to be so proper and respectable? People who were born to live splendid lives in this world, and people who weren't – I wonder if the distinction wasn't there from the beginning."

"Well, I'm just a blockhead, but . . ."

"But what?"

He's studying my face with a strange look in his eyes, like an actual madman. I hesitate, unable to respond. The thought of saying anything real and specific is too horrifying.

"But . . . When you're in pain, it hurts me too."

"What the hell? Don't be stupid," he says, but smiles as if relieved.

At this moment, for the first time in I don't know how

long, I feel a fresh sense of well-being wash over me. (That's it: if I put my husband at ease, I too will feel more at ease. It's not about morality or anything of the sort; if you feel at ease, you're doing fine.)

Late that night, I slip beneath my husband's mosquito netting.

"It's all right. Everything's all right," I tell him, collapsing on the mat next to his futon. "I'm not bothered."

"*Excuse me,*" he says in English, half-jokingly butchering the words in a husky voice. Then he slips out of his futon, sits on the tatami facing me, and adds, again in English, "*Not to worry!*"

The summer moon is full tonight, and four or five silver slivers of moonbeam pierce the cracks in the rain shutters, penetrate the netting, and impale his sunken, naked chest.

"You're getting so skinny," I tell him, smiling and half joking in return. He repositions himself, sitting up straighter, and says, "You're skinnier too. You worry too much, that's why."

"No. Didn't I just tell you? I'm not bothered. It's all right. I'm a smart girl. But . . . if you'd just show me that you appreciate me now and then. . ."

He laughs, predictably, when I say this, but his expression soon turns serious.

"I do appreciate you, and I believe I show you that.

Whichever way the wind blows, I appreciate you. You're a truly good person. Stop worrying about silly things, be proud of who you are, and relax. The truth is that you are *all* I think about, so, as far as that goes, you should have all the confidence in the world."

He declares this in an awfully formal way, dampening the mood again and putting me in an awkward position.

"But you ... You've changed," I say quietly, head bowed.

(I'd rather you didn't think about me at all! It would actually be easier on my feelings if you hated and despised me. You say you think about me all the time, yet you're embracing another woman. Envisioning that is enough to plunge me straight into hell. I wonder if men are under the mistaken impression that simply thinking about their wives makes them paragons of morality. Do they believe that even if they find someone else to love, they can remain righteous and virtuous as long as they don't forget about their wives? Is that what it means to be a man? If they fall in love with another woman, then proceed to sit around in front of their wives, agonizing over moral dilemmas and sighing gloomily, that gloom is bound to rub off on the wife, and she too will begin sighing. Let the husband maintain an easygoing, lighthearted attitude, on the other hand, and the wife won't have to go through hell. If you love someone else, forget all about your wife, and simply love that someone without reservation or guilt.)

He chuckles feebly and says, "Change? Not me. It's just that it's been so hot recently. I can't take the heat. All I have to say about summer is, *No thank you!*"

I don't know what to do with that, so I too chuckle. "Such a vexatious man," I say, lightly slapping his shoulder. Then I exit the mosquito netting, go to my own room, duck under the netting there, and lie down between my son and baby daughter.

I'm happy that I was able to feel that close to my husband even for those few minutes, to share a laugh with him. I feel as if some of the pressure inside me has been released, and for the first time in quite a while I get a full, untroubled night's sleep.

I hope we can go along just like this from now on, being casually affectionate with each other, joking together, letting even deceptions slide, and not always worrying about the proper attitude to take. All that "morality" business doesn't really matter. I want to feel at ease in life, if only a little bit, and if only for a short time. An hour or two of real enjoyment is enough, according to this new outlook, and one morning, just as cheerful laughter has begun once again to be a regular feature in our home, my husband announces his intention to visit a hot springs resort.

"These headaches are killing me. It's the heat. I have

an acquaintance who lives near that *onsen* in Shinshu, and he told me to drop in anytime, no need to bring anything, not even food, he says. I want to spend two or three weeks there, have a proper rest. The way things are going, I'm about to lose my mind. I need to get away from Tokyo."

I wonder for a moment if what he needs to get away from isn't that other woman.

"What shall I do if an armed robber breaks in while you're away?" I say this with a big smile. (Yes, sad people always smile a lot.)

"Here's what you tell him. You say, 'My husband is a madman.' Even armed robbers are no match for lunatics."

I have no reason to oppose the trip, so I go to the closet to grab his expensive new linen kimono, only to find that it isn't there – or anywhere else I look.

"It's gone," I tell him, feeling sick inside. "What could have happened to it? A cat burglar, maybe?"

"I sold it."

He says this with a twisted smile that more closely resembles an attempt to hold back tears.

I'm aghast but try not to show it.

"My. So impulsive."

"That's what makes me more dangerous than any pistol-packing burglar."

I have to assume he needed extra money to help out the woman.

"Well, what are you going to wear, then?"

"A single open-neck shirt will do me."

He announced the trip in the morning, and by noon he's ready to set out. It seems he wants to escape this house at the earliest possible moment. Tokyo has been sunny and stiflingly hot day after day, but today we have a rare rain shower. My husband sits on the step above the entrance, with shoes already on his feet and a rucksack on his back. He's scowling at the rain, impatiently willing it to stop, when he abruptly mutters, "I wonder if crape myrtles only bloom every other year."

This year, the crape myrtle at our front entrance hasn't put out a single flower.

"It looks that way," is my vague reply. And that's the last snatch of intimate conversation I'll ever have with my husband.

The rain stops, and he sets out on his trip in a hurry, as if fleeing. Three days later, a short article appears in the paper about a double suicide at Lake Suwa. A couple of days after that, I receive my husband's farewell letter, sent from his inn at the lake.

"It's not for love that I die with this woman. I'm a journalist. A journalist entices others to revolution and subversion while he himself slips away, flicking the cowardly sweat from his brow. He's a truly ghastly creature. A modern-day demon. Unable to bear the self-hatred any longer, I decided of my own free will to mount the revolutionary's cross. A journalist caught in a scandal of his own – is that not a first? I only hope my death can help in some small way to force all other ghastly modern-day demons to blush and repent."

And so on – the letter was full of truly ridiculous, idiotic sentiments like this. Do men need to put on such airs, obsessing over the significance of heaven knows what and spewing pretentious lies, until the very moment of death?

According to a friend of my husband's who came by to pay his respects, the woman was a twenty-eight-year-old reporter for the magazine publisher in Kanda; while I was taking shelter in Aomori she had often stayed at our house, and there was something about a pregnancy. But to explain dying at his own hand by raving about revolution and heaven knows what . . . My husband was just no good, I'm convinced of that now.

Revolutions are fought with the intention of making life better for people. I put no faith in revolutionaries who see themselves as tragic heroes. Why couldn't he go ahead and enjoy his love for that woman more openly? I suppose he wasn't capable of loving her in a way that would spill over into happier times for me, his wife. The suffering of the individual must be great, but a man's hellish love affair is, first and foremost, a nightmare for those around him.

To master your feelings and quietly turn your own world around is the true revolution. If you can do that, you'll find no problem too difficult to handle. Unable to alter the way he felt about his wife, my husband's appalling choice was the "revolutionary's cross."

I take the train with all three children to collect their father's remains in Suwa, and on the way I can't stop trembling – not with sorrow or anger so much as disgust at the absolute idiocy of it all.

# AN ENTERTAINING LADY

Madam has always seemed to enjoy taking special care of guests, serving them delicious meals and so forth, but I'm tempted to say it's not so much that she's *fond* of guests as that she's terrified of them. When I go to her room to announce a visitor, she looks as tense as a small bird about to take flight to elude a swooping eagle. She's fixing loose locks of hair and straightening the folds of her kimono as she rises to her feet, and before I've even finished my announcement she's trotting down the corridor to the entryway to greet the visitor in a curious, high-pitched, flutelike squeal that somehow seems to both laugh and weep at the same time. Her gaze takes on an almost deranged intensity as she dashes madly back and forth between the kitchen and the living room, overturning pots, breaking dishes, and apologizing repeatedly to me, the maid. And then, once the guests have gone, she plops down on a cushion in the living room and slumps there, too exhausted to help with the cleanup, her eyes sometimes brimming with tears.

Madam's husband was a professor at the university in Hongo. He'd been born into a wealthy family, and I guess the madam comes from a rich farming family in Fukushima; and perhaps it has something to do with not having had any children, but they were very much like innocent children themselves, happy and carefree. I was hired to help out in this house four years ago, when we were still at war, and about six months later the professor, though he was physically infirm and classified as a second-class militiaman, was suddenly drafted into the army and apparently had the misfortune of being deployed to the South Pacific. Though the war ended soon after that, his whereabouts are still unknown, and his commanding officer sent Madam a plain postcard to the effect that it might be best if she resigned herself to assuming the worst. Ever since then, Madam's fervor for entertaining guests has turned into something like a mania, and has resulted in many tragic scenes I can scarcely bear to watch.

Before Dr. Sasajima appeared, however, Madam's socializing was more or less confined to her in-laws and her own relatives. Even after her husband was sent to the South Pacific, her family back home in Fukushima provided her with a substantial allowance, so that she was living a life of quiet ease, a refined life, if you will.

But once Dr. Sasajima started showing up, everything went straight to hell.

This property is outside of Tokyo proper, though with easy access to the city, and fortunately the house suffered no damage in the war. People from the city who were bombed out of house and home have flooded the area, however, to the extent that, walking through the shopping district, it feels as if all the familiar faces have been switched out, replaced with an entirely different cast of characters.

It was the end of last year, I believe, that Madam was at the market and ran into her husband's old friend Dr. Sasajima, for the first time in some ten years, and brought him to the house. That's when our luck turned bad.

Dr. Sasajima was about the same age as the professor, forty or so, and was also a professor at the same university, although attached to the medical school, whereas my employer had been in the literature department. The two of them had also been classmates in middle school, apparently. At some point, before building this house, the professor and Madam lived briefly in a building in Komagome where Dr. Sasajima, still a bachelor, also rented an apartment, and during that short period of time they were quite close friends, but after the professor moved here, what with their fields of research being unrelated, they hadn't had any contact during the past ten-plus years. And then the doctor happened to see Madam at the market in our town and called out to her. Rather than just exchanging greetings and moving on, as she should have done, her hospitality mania got the best of her, and she blurted out that her home was only a short distance away, so, please, come have a look, what's your hurry, and so on, not actually wanting to detain the man, I'm sure, but desperately trying to do so anyway. What is that? A frenzied overreaction to her own terror of guests? Dr. Sasajima, quite a sight with his shopping basket and inverness cape, allowed himself to be led to the house.

"Whoa! Pretty nice place you've got here. No war damage at all, then? Lucky you. You aren't living with anyone else, I guess. Seems kind of wasteful. Then again, it's difficult to ask for lodging in a house with no man, especially one as spotless and refined as this; a male lodger would end up feeling awfully constrained. But seriously, Missus, I had no idea you were living so near. I'd heard that your house was in this town, but, well, people can be awfully oblivious; I landed here almost a year ago now, and I always use this street on my way to and from the market, but I never noticed the nameplate on your gate. Me, I was drafted into the army shortly after my marriage, and when I finally made it back I found my house burned to the ground. My wife had taken our boy, who was born while I was away, and evacuated to her family home in

Chiba. I'd like to bring her back to Tokyo, but I have no house, and no choice but to stay on here alone, renting a three-mat room behind the general store, cooking my own meals. Tonight I thought I'd make myself a chicken stew and drink myself blind, which is why I was wandering around the market dangling this stupid shopping basket. Desperation – that's about all I've been left with. I'm not even sure if I'm dead or alive."

Sitting on a cushion in the living room, knees spread wide, he carries on exclusively about himself.

"You poor man," says Madam, as her reactive hospitality mania begins taking hold. She comes trotting into the kitchen with that odd gleam in her eye and says, "Ume-chan, *sumimasen*," apologizing to me again before asking me to prepare a pot of chicken stew and warm the sake, then spinning on her heel and scurrying back to the living room, only to reappear in a flash to light the fire and set out the cups and dishes. It's the same as always, but this time I see the mixture of excitement, anxiety, and agitation as not just pathetic but infuriating.

Dr. Sasajima now shamelessly bellows: "What's that you say? Chicken stew? If I may say so, Missus, I always like konjac noodles in my chicken stew, so if you could throw in some of those . . . Oh, and also, if you have any fried tofu, that would be fantastic. Onions alone is just sad, right?"

Before he's even finished speaking, Madam comes tumbling into the kitchen.

"Ume-chan, sumimasen."

She looks somewhat embarrassed, but also like a baby about to bawl.

Dr. Sasajima, having declared it a pain to drink from a little sake cup, guzzles from a tea mug instead and is soon drunk.

"Is that so. Your husband's fate is still unknown? Well, eight or nine times out of ten that means he died in the war. It can't be helped, Missus, you're not the only one who's suffered misfortune, you know."

He quickly disposes of her feelings and gets right back to his favorite subject.

"Look at me," he says. "No house to live in, separated from my dear wife and child. All our worldly possessions went up in smoke with the house, even our clothing and futons and mosquito nets. I'm left with absolutely nothing. Before moving into that three-mat room behind the general store, I was bedding down in a hallway at the university hospital. The doctors there are living in conditions far worse than their patients. Almost makes you wish you were a patient yourself. No, it's terrible. Miserable. You're one of the lucky ones."

"Yes, that's true," Madam is quick to agree. "Compared to most people, I'm almost too blessed. I often think that."

"That's right. So true. Next time I'll bring some friends of mine who, these fellows, all of 'em have suffered the worst kind of luck, so, really, I mean, I have no choice but to rely on your generosity and compassion."

Madam chuckles as if delighted and says, "Well, of course," then adds, more solemnly, "It would be an honor."

And ever since that day, our home has been a virtual hell.

It turned out not to be just some joking, drunken bluster. Four or five days later, what do you know? The professor brazenly shows up with three of his friends in tow. "Today," he announces, "we had our year-end party at the hospital, and now we're going to have the after-party here at your house, I know you don't mind. We'll be drinking late into the night, because, I mean, we haven't had a place to hold our after-parties for quite a while now, and it's been a real problem, but, hey! Come on in, friends, make yourselves at home, the living room is this way, don't worry about your coats, you can leave 'em on, it's freezing in here . . ." And so on, barking and bellowing and acting as if he owns the place. One of his friends is a woman, a nurse apparently, and right there in front of everyone he's fooling around with her, all the while ordering Madam about, as if she were his servant. Madam just titters nervously and does as he says.

"Missus, sorry, but could you light the *kotatsu* for us? And if you could just handle the drinks, like last time. Don't worry if you have no sake – *shochu* or whiskey will do. Oh, and as for eats, I almost forgot, tonight I brought you a special gift, broiled eel, wait till you try this. This is the stuff you want when it's cold outside. One skewer for you, Missus, and one for the rest of us, shall we say, and also, hey, who was it who had that apple? Don't be stingy, hand it over to the Missus here. It's called an Indo apple, Missus, very sweet, incredible fragrance."

As I'm carrying the tea tray into the living room, an apple, fresh from someone's pocket, rolls across the table top, falls to the floor, and comes to rest at my feet. I wish I could give it a mighty kick. A single apple. To even call that a gift is beyond brazen. As for the slices of eel, they're squished flat and half dried out and look almost inedible.

Madam is bullied into drinking all night with this rowdy crew, and with the first pale glow of dawn, they all sack out on the floor surrounding the kotatsu, legs tucked under the quilt to capture the warmth of the heated pit. Madam is more or less forced to join them. I'm sure she hasn't slept a wink, but the others snore away until well past noon. When they finally get up, notably dispirited now that they're no longer drunk, each of them has a bowl of cooked rice and tea. They avoid making eye contact with me, as I've stopped trying to disguise my anger, and before long they file out, looking like a string of half-drowned rats.

"Madam, why in the world would you sleep on the floor with that crowd? Such behavior is appalling to me."

"I'm sorry. I just can't bring myself to say no."

Seeing her pale, exhausted, sleep-deprived face and the tears welling up in her eyes, I'm unable to say any more.

The attacks of these wolves just gets worse and worse, turning this house into something like a dormitory for Dr. Sasajima's comrades. Sometimes his friends come without him and stay the night, pressing their hostess to bed down on the floor with all of them. Madam alone gets no sleep; she's not a physically robust person to begin with, and now, when the house is free of pests, she spends whole days in bed.

"Madam, you look so fatigued. You have to stop associating with those people."

"Forgive me, Ume-chan. I just can't. They've all had so much misfortune and unhappiness in life. Gathering here is probably the only fun they get to have."

Ridiculous. Meanwhile, Madam's financial situation grows more uncertain; it seems that, at this rate, she may have to sell the house in the coming year. In front of guests, however, she never gives so much as a hint that she has any such concerns whatsoever. Though her health is clearly declining, whenever visitors arrive she springs out of bed, fixes her hair and kimono in a flash, trots to the entrance, and welcomes them in that strange squeal, half laugh and half sob.

It's a night in early spring. We have, unsurprisingly, a pair of drunken visitors. "It'll be another late night," Madam says, "so let's hurry up and eat something now, before we get too busy." The two of us stand there in the kitchen stuffing ourselves with steamed buns. Madam serves the guests all kinds of delicious foods, while for her solitary dinner she makes do with a single steamed bun.

As we were eating, we heard a roar of vulgar, drunken laughter issuing from the living room, followed by:

"Now, now, don't give me that. I have my suspicions about you. Even a woman like this one, she's ..." The rest of the sentence was like poison to the ears – an unbelievably filthy and disrespectful sentiment, delivered in medical terms.

To which came a response in the voice of young Dr. Imai:

"What're you talking about? I'm not here for romance. To me, this is just a place to lay my head."

Furious, I look up at Madam.

She's standing under the dim electric light, head bowed, silently eating her steamed bun. Her eyes, understandably enough, glitter with tears. I feel so sorry for her, I can't find any words.

Madam, head still bowed, says in a quiet voice, "Ume-chan, if you wouldn't mind, please heat the bath tomorrow morning. Dr. Imai loves his morning bath."

This might be the only time I've seen her face reveal true indignation. But afterwards she acts as if nothing untoward has happened at all, flashing gay smiles at the guests and scurrying frantically back and forth between kitchen and living room.

It's obvious to me that her health is declining, but when she's entertaining guests she tries not to let it show. Most of the visitors are prominent doctors, and yet somehow not a single one of them seems to have divined the actual state of her health.

It's a quiet morning in spring, with fortunately not a single overnight guest present. I'm at the well, idly washing some clothing, when Madam staggers out into the garden in her bare feet, crouches down near the flowering hedge, and coughs up a considerable volume of blood. I cry out and run to her, wrap my arms around her from behind, and all but carry her to her room, where I lay her gently down. And then, sobbing, I let it all out.

"See? That's why I hate these guests! They're all doctors, right? Now that it's come to this, I'm going to demand that they restore your health or ... or face my wrath!"

"No, no, you mustn't say anything of the sort to our guests. They might feel responsible, or guilty."

"But look how ill you are! What are you going to do now? Continue to jump out of bed and entertain all comers? Cough up blood while you're sleeping on the floor with them? That'll make a fine spectacle."

Madam closes her eyes and thinks for a few moments.

"I'll just go back to my family home for now. Ume-chan, I'll need you to watch over things while I'm gone, and I insist that you continue to allow guests to spend the night. Those poor people have no homes of their own to relax in. And no, you may not tell anyone about my condition."

After these stern instructions, she favors me with a gentle smile.

I begin packing her luggage right away. As I'm doing so, I decide I need to accompany her to Fukushima, so I run to the station and purchase two train tickets. We're to leave in three days.

When the morning of our departure arrives, Madam is feeling considerably better. Hoping to escape before any visitors show up, I keep pressing her to hurry. I close all the rain shutters and lock the door behind us, and just as we turn to leave,

"Hallelujah!"

It's Dr. Sasajima, drunk as a lord in broad daylight, with two young women in tow.

"Hello! Were you going somewhere?" he asks.

"No, no," says Madam. "Nowhere important. Ume-chan, forgive me, but can you open the shutters in the living room? Come in, Doctor, please. It's no inconvenience at all."

With that strange, high-pitched, laughing-or-weeping voice, she welcomes the young ladies as well and then begins scurrying about like a frightened mouse, eager as always to serve the guests while she sends me out to buy provisions.

At the market, when I go to pay, I find that in her frenzied haste, Madam handed me not her wallet but her travel handbook. There's a large bill inside, but the first thing I see when I open it is her train ticket, torn in two. I'm shocked at this, and at the realization that she must have destroyed it the moment Dr. Sasajima called out to us. Stunned at the depths of her selflessness, her willingness to sacrifice herself for others, I feel as though, for the first time in my life, I've discovered something truly sacred and precious, something that we human beings, alone of all creatures, possess. I fish my own ticket out of my obi and rip it in two, and then, reflecting that the more delicious treats we have at home, the better, I go back to scouring the market.

# New Directions Paperbooks—a partial listing

Denise Levertov, Selected Poems
Li Po, Selected Poems
Clarice Lispector, An Apprenticeship
  The Hour of the Star
  The Passion According to G. H.
Federico García Lorca, Selected Poems*
Nathaniel Mackey, Splay Anthem
Xavier de Maistre, Voyage Around My Room
Stéphane Mallarmé, Selected Poetry and Prose*
Javier Marías, Your Face Tomorrow (3 volumes)
Bernadette Mayer, Midwinter Day
Carson McCullers, The Member of the Wedding
Fernando Melchor, Hurricane Season
  Paradais
Thomas Merton, New Seeds of Contemplation
  The Way of Chuang Tzu
Henri Michaux, A Barbarian in Asia
Henry Miller, The Colossus of Maroussi
  Big Sur & the Oranges of Hieronymus Bosch
Yukio Mishima, Confessions of a Mask
  Death in Midsummer
Eugenio Montale, Selected Poems*
Vladimir Nabokov, Laughter in the Dark
Pablo Neruda, The Captain's Verses*
  Love Poems*
Charles Olson, Selected Writings
George Oppen, New Collected Poems
Wilfred Owen, Collected Poems
Hiroko Oyamada, The Hole
José Emilio Pacheco, Battles in the Desert
Michael Palmer, Little Elegies for Sister Satan
Nicanor Parra, Antipoems*
Boris Pasternak, Safe Conduct
Octavio Paz, Poems of Octavio Paz
Victor Pelevin, Omon Ra
Fernando Pessoa
  The Complete Works of Alberto Caeiro
Alejandra Pizarnik
  Extracting the Stone of Madness
Robert Plunket, My Search for Warren Harding
Ezra Pound, The Cantos
  New Selected Poems and Translations
Qian Zhongshu, Fortress Besieged
Raymond Queneau, Exercises in Style
Olga Ravn, The Employees
Herbert Read, The Green Child
Kenneth Rexroth, Selected Poems
Keith Ridgway, A Shock

Rainer Maria Rilke
  Poems from the Book of Hours
Arthur Rimbaud, Illuminations*
  A Season in Hell and The Drunken Boat*
Evelio Rosero, The Armies
Fran Ross, Oreo
Joseph Roth, The Emperor's Tomb
Raymond Roussel, Locus Solus
Ihara Saikaku, The Life of an Amorous Woman
Nathalie Sarraute, Tropisms
Jean-Paul Sartre, Nausea
Kathryn Scanlan, Kick the Latch
Delmore Schwartz
  In Dreams Begin Responsibilities
W. G. Sebald, The Emigrants
  The Rings of Saturn
Anne Serre, The Governesses
Patti Smith, Woolgathering
Stevie Smith, Best Poems
  Novel on Yellow Paper
Gary Snyder, Turtle Island
Muriel Spark, The Driver's Seat
  The Public Image
Maria Stepanova, In Memory of Memory
Wislawa Szymborska, How to Start Writing
Antonio Tabucchi, Pereira Maintains
Junichiro Tanizaki, The Maids
Yoko Tawada, The Emissary
  Scattered All over the Earth
Dylan Thomas, A Child's Christmas in Wales
  Collected Poems
Thuan, Chinatown
Rosemary Tonks, The Bloater
Tomas Tranströmer, The Great Enigma
Leonid Tsypkin, Summer in Baden-Baden
Tu Fu, Selected Poems
Elio Vittorini, Conversations in Sicily
Rosmarie Waldrop, The Nick of Time
Robert Walser, The Tanners
Eliot Weinberger, An Elemental Thing
  Nineteen Ways of Looking at Wang Wei
Nathanael West, The Day of the Locust
  Miss Lonelyhearts
Tennessee Williams, The Glass Menagerie
  A Streetcar Named Desire
William Carlos Williams, Selected Poems
Alexis Wright, Praiseworthy
Louis Zukofsky, "A"

*BILINGUAL EDITION

For a complete listing, request a free catalog from New Directions, 80 8th Avenue, New York, NY 10011
or visit us online at ndbooks.com